STONE WALL FREEDOM

FREEDOM

The Pirate

*A fictional story inspired by the beauty
and history of Block Island, RI*

STONE WALL FREEDOM

The Pirate

*A fictional story inspired by the beauty
and history of Block Island, RI*

DAVID LEE TUCKER

Two Harbors Press
212 3rd Avenue North, Suite 290
Minneapolis, MN 55401
612.455.2293
www.TwoHarborsPress.com

ISBN - 978-1-936198-28-3
ISBN - 1-936198-28-2
LCCN - 2010932353

Book design by Wendy Arakawa
Cover art by Eleni Tucker

Printed in the United States of America

Acknowledgements

I thank my talented wife, Eleni, for her beautiful artistry that effectively coaxed this story out of me.
In remembrance, I thank my father, Joe "Gid" Tucker, for his legacy of passionate love for Block Island.
Finally, I would like to extend my gratitude to all of those who have taken an interest and encouraged me to continue writing throughout this long journey.

TGBTG

Foreword

In the spring of 1967, my family set out on an expedition to study the Connecticut, Rhode Island, and Massachusetts shorelines, looking for our place in the summer sun. The trip, as fate would have it, included a short ferry ride to a small, distant land surrounded by water called Block Island.

Once on the island, we were swept off in an old station wagon by an even older cabby to take the obligatory tour. That tour started a love affair that has continued for several generations. At the age of twelve, my only recollections of that visit were of the Mohegan Bluffs, stories of colonial pioneers, Revolutionary patriots, pirate treasure, and, most intriguing, a story of slaves and stone walls.

When my parents offhandedly commented about the numerous stone walls dotting the island landscape, our cabby gave an explanation that has stayed with me to this day. He said that slaves had built many of the walls, and that any slave who completed a wall that crossed from one side of the island to the other could earn his freedom. The idea caught my imagination and settled somewhere in the recesses of my mind. Since that time, I have heard the story of the stone walls repeated to reinforce this lore, legend, or myth. It was more than thirty years later, while admiring a Block Island landscape painted by my wife, that a story started to emerge from its hiding place in the back of my mind.

The same questions began to circle in my mind again as they had in that cab over thirty years earlier. This was not the Deep South. Did slave ownership actually exist in the Northeast? Were slaves really on the island, and did they, in fact, build the stone walls? When would this have taken place? If there were slaves, why would an ordinance or declaration offering slaves their freedom in exchange for stone walls have been adopted?

As for pirates, was there any basis in truth for the stories of pirate treasure, or were they just concoctions to drum up tourist business?

Pirates and Treasure

Due to its location, Block Island has a history filled with pirate lore and legend. Names like Joseph Brandish, "Black Sam" Bellamy, the wretched scoundrel Edward Low, and the infamous Captain Kidd were all active in and around Block Island. Some of the island's own sons apparently joined pirate crews in search of fortune. Also, the pirate Paulsgrave Williams came from a family of Block Island landowners.

It is well documented that Kidd visited Block Island while returning from an Indian Ocean voyage. Kidd had left New England on legitimate business for the Crown, but at some point, he turned to engaging in outlaw piracy. When Kidd returned, he distributed his booty in locations around the Long Island and Block Island Sounds before going to meet one of his patrons in Boston. Kidd was apprehended, sent to England, and eventually hanged. The proximity of the island, as well as the documented evidence regarding pirate visits to it, provides a wealth of reasons to speculate that privateers and pirates alike may have left treasure buried on Block Island.

Stone Walls and Slaves

Throughout New England, over the years, the rocky soil was cleared to plant crops, and the rocks were piled up as boundary markers in the form of stone walls. In S. T. Livermore's book, *History of Block Island*, published in 1877, he describes the soil found by the early islanders as follows:

> *When they landed on the island, it must have been difficult in some places to have missed stepping on a stone. A glance at the walls now standing is evidence enough that before they were built the surface of the ground was well-nigh paved with small bowlders. It is no exaggeration to say that more than three hundred miles of stone-wall now constitutes the fences of Block Island . . . While they so frequently disturbed the plow and the hoe of the pioneers, few, perhaps, thought of their value in future ages to fence the fields after the primitive forests had disappeared.*

It must have taken a huge effort to clear the land for plantation farming and the pasturage that was created at that time. The extraordinary number of walls is evidence to that. It is believed that many of these stone walls date as far back as the 1600s.

If slaves did inhabit Block Island, is it unreasonable to think that their labor was used to clear the fields and build the walls? There are records from southern Rhode Island that substantiate that this job was typically relegated to slaves. I asked myself, was that the task that the owners or even paid employees would have done if slave labor were available?

From the 1600s through 1774, Newport, Rhode Island, may have been one of the busiest ports engaging in slave trade in the North American British colonies. Also, during the same time period up to the Revolutionary War, a plantation system of farming existed in southern Rhode Island. According to the *World Book Encyclopedia*:

It somewhat resembled the plantation system of the south. The islands in Narragansett Bay and the coastal regions, known as Narragansett Country, were fertile and well adapted for grazing. Many wealthy planters had farms of 1,000 acres or more, and owned slaves who tilled the land and cared for horses, sheep, and cattle. The plantations produced great quantities of cheese for export.

In fact, the preamble to the Rhode Island Constitution, adopted in 1842, refers to the people of the "State of Rhode Island and Providence Plantations." This can still be found on some state letterheads. The original records of the purchase and settlement of the island by investors and settlers indicated that it was for the purpose of establishing a "plantation." Apparently, over the years, property had always been bought and sold quite frequently, but in the early 1700s, the island had consolidated into three regions, each having unique owners, people, and plantation life. John "Ed" Littlefield, a nineteenth-century island editorialist and reviewer of Livermore's book, wrote:

According to Livermore the early proprietors of the Island, Simon Ray, on the West Side, James Sands, near the Center, and Thomas Terry on Indian Head Neck, all lived on a grand scale with slaves and servants to run their extensive farms and large houses. They entertained many notables, and were socially intimate with many mainland families of consequence and means.

The first U.S. census of 1790 revealed that there were forty-seven slaves on Block Island. Although slave trade was first ruled illegal in 1774 by Rhode Island courts, and emancipation legislation was slowly being adopted, it was not until 1842, with the ratification of their constitution, that slavery was officially abolished altogether. It was another twenty years later that the ongoing agitation between the North and the South culminated in the outbreak of civil war in 1861.

There are few documented references to substantiate that slaves built the stone walls, let alone earned their freedom in this way. However, in her *Block Island Scrapbook*, published in 1957, Mary Elizabeth Hyde referenced the story by saying that many of the stone walls were built by slaves, and then stated that four slaves actually achieved the goal and were set free, though there are no historical records to verify that this actually happened. While knowledge of the story is mixed among the islanders, there are those who always assumed this story to be true. Fact or fiction, this story continues to be propagated—but only through oral history and tradition.

The questions of why and when are inextricably coupled together. The period of the late 1700s or early 1800s would seem to have been ripe for such events. The increased awareness of personal freedom as a result of the war for independence—and the growing activity of Christian church leaders and abolitionists in the North—resulted in the adoption of various pieces of emancipation legislation.

The emancipation that gradually occurred, however, was not driven by the legislation but by growing social pressure. The pressures came not only from outside forces but, most likely, from the slaves themselves. Because of the struggle for freedom that was going on around them, the slaves may have become more assertive about their own personal freedom.

What greater motivation could there have been than to create an incentive that addressed both the islanders' need to clear the fields and the slaves' greatest desire: freedom? The strong work ethic of the islanders of the day might have combined with these influences to suggest that freedom could be achieved, but the slaves would have to earn it.

Why, then, is there no record of this ever occurring? The answer may be that while slaves had been building the stone walls for years, any such "ordinance" may have been in effect for a very short time. Or it could have been that this occurred in the form of a few individual "manumissions", or written documents, freeing a slave for good service to the master who had this particular stipulation. Regardless, it is likely that few, if any, were ever able to accomplish the task and earn their freedom in this way.

Without any evidence to support if or when this may have happened, we can speculate that this could have taken place during the gradual emancipation period from before the start of the Revolutionary War in 1776 and the adoption of the Rhode Island law abolishing slavery in 1842. Based on the changing social and moral values in the North during that period, records show that growing numbers of slave owners, either voluntarily or under social pressure, provided for manumissions to a status of indentured servants or to full emancipation.

Block Islanders

In Arthur Kinoy's published paper "The Real Mystery of Block Island — The Origins of the Island Colony," he concludes that the first settlers came to Block Island to escape Puritan religious persecution. They came to settle a land where they could freely live out the convictions of their Christian faith. The resulting form of town government is thought to have been the first real democracy established in America. A wealth of evidence indicates that the island settlers and residents throughout the years have been good, decent, hard-working, patriotic, and God-fearing people.

Some town hall records on Block Island from the late 1700s admonish masters for mistreatment of slaves, giving some indication that systematic abusive treatment was unlikely at that time. The vision of bullwhips and the stereotypical brutality of the Southern plantations in the 1800s likely was not the reality for most slaves in southern Rhode Island and Block Island. Slaves in the North could hold property and had a legal right to life.

There are indications that during this period, slaves were treated with some level of Christian dignity, beyond the status of a mere "possession". There remains the possibility that they were treated more as servants or, in some cases, almost as a part of the family. In fact, many slaves were typically identified as "members" of the slave owner's family. Still, slavery in the Northeast was a harsh system, providing living conditions that were consistently substandard. It demeaned human beings as possessions who were not afforded the same freedoms as other human beings.

Block Island

There may be no more mystical or magical place on this earth than an island, and perhaps even more so, a small island. What is it that draws men to her soil? The seventeenth-century English writer and preacher John Donne wrote the famous words, "No man is an island, entire of itself." The spiritual truth in that statement is also an indication that there is no greater test to a man's adventurous spirit, indomitable character, and unwavering faith than to make his home upon one. Why would those first pioneers choose this small island while so much rich, virgin territory lay west of them on the mainland?

As an island, it is set apart by water and weather, with limited resources and little hope for rescue or help in time of trouble. Its clearly defined boundaries, its communion with the sea, and its independence said to those most stout pioneers, "Make me home, and I will make you men among men!" Those first families who pushed their cattle off the barges to swim to shore in full sight of natives who had killed white visitors before them embodied the greatest of pioneer qualities.

It was very likely that slavery in the 1700s was an invaluable source of labor that freed the Founding Fathers to engage in the great revolutionary struggle. Is it possible that their God could have used those enslaved men and women against the very system that enslaved them? Did their contributions help to create a nation founded upon ideals that would cause her people to face the inevitable job of tearing down their own system of slavery? The finished product of true freedom from prejudice and bigotry has been a long work in progress which continues to be one of the measuring sticks that determines just how free a nation we really are.

The people of Block Island, as part of the great state of Rhode Island, should take pride in the fact that they were the first to abolish the business of trading in slaves, even before they were the first colony to declare war on England. Both were giant steps in long struggles ahead.

Stone Wall Freedom—The Pirate is part one of a three-part fictional tale inspired by the beauty and history of Block Island, using S. T. Livermore's *The History of Block Island* as the primary historical resource. The entire story was written as a tribute to the microcosm of the struggle for freedom that the men and women, both free and slave, faced on this blessed little land.

Part One

Chapter One

The Spanish crew huddled together, held captive on the deck of their own ship. By quick count, First Mate Darby Blackbury reported to his captain that there were "'bout four dozen Spanish in numba, sah."

It was the year of grace 1749, and Captain Giddy Gilcox, the last of the great Caribbean pirates, continued to wreak havoc with trade throughout the Americas. Gilcox, along with his first mate and quartermaster, stood fast on deck of the Spanish galley while his bosun rummaged below in search of valuables.

Gilcox watched his pirate crew move about cautiously and more nervously than usual. A sense of chilling portent had run up his own spine as soon as he had stepped aboard this ship. The wretched cries from below deck unnerved his normally cold-blooded heart. He knew his crew felt it, too. They had never scuttled a slave ship before. Though he would never admit it, he, like his crew, would just as soon be off her cursed timbers.

The Spanish captain had already been taken to his cabin to unlock the chest that housed his valuables. His only value now to Gilcox was as an example to the remaining Spanish crew of Gilcox's brutish authority.

"Bring the honorable captain before me," Gilcox commanded in unpolished King's English. The pirates dragged the struggling Spanish captain to Gilcox and forced him to his knees. It was a drama they had played out many times before.

"There is but one captain aboard any one ship," Gilcox calmly announced as he slowly drew his short, razor-sharp sword. With three quick thrusts, he strategically slashed the man's throat and stuck him twice in the abdomen. The blood poured out of the Spaniard as he dropped to the deck, writhing in pain.

This act had always proven to remove the last ounce of fight that might be left in any Spanish crew, and Gilcox knew this crew would respond no differently. Most of them stood, but a few knelt and quietly murmured desperate prayers to the Blessed Mother. Their hands were tied behind their backs, all bound together on one cord like a string of dark pearls, with their sweat glistening in the morning sun.

Bodies of their mates lay scattered across the bloodstained deck as the ship gently rocked in the steadily rolling sea. These were able-bodied, seafaring men, but fear weakened their sea legs. The whole group flopped back and forth with the ship as they tried to steady themselves against each other.

Gilcox loomed before them, searching their faces. He wondered, *Will any more dare to sneak another horrified glance at me?* He hated and despised those who looked upon him and showed any sign of repulsion. It had become something of a game to the pirate. For those who dared, Gilcox would nod to one of his crew, and the offender would immediately be stabbed or bludgeoned to death.

He whispered to himself, almost disappointedly, "No more takers today." He continued, saying aloud to the Spanish crew, "I know what you're thinking. I hear your murmurs—'*La Cara del Diablo*.' You dirty Spanish dogs may think that this is merely the face of the devil, but the truth you will soon find is that you have actually just met the devil himself."

Giddy Gilcox had a peculiar fascination with his own ghastly appearance. There was a time when he could not stand the sight of himself. These days, he searched for his reflection in mirrors with growing admiration. He treasured his visage that struck such fear within the hearts of men.

Stricken by a mysterious ailment as a child, his face was left gaunt and scarred. With dark sunken cheeks and eyes, a razor-thin nose, and a sharp chin, he resembled a living skull. His contorted lips exposed the few remaining large, discolored teeth still in his mouth. The state of his skin left him with a constant red rash and warts that were strung together in lines up and down his body. It looked as though a red candle had melted on the very top of his head and dripped down his face. The condition of his skin didn't allow him to grow a beard to cover these features, and his hair only grew in small patches here and there.

Another wave of fear and repulsion rolled through the Spanish crew, but it wasn't directed at Gilcox. The pirate ship's doctor and cook, "Digits" Baxendale, was moving from body to body of the Spaniards' dead shipmates, collecting "souvenirs" from each. These included gully knives, gold earrings, rings—and something that caused many of the Spaniards to grow faint: Digits, using sharp shears like those used by ship surgeons, was removing the index fingers from each body and carefully storing them in a canvas bag.

The pirate captain thought back to the first time he had seen Digits in action. Neither he nor any of his crew quite understood this strange hobby, but he quickly realized that this activity also served other purposes. First, it served as a bit of entertainment. The crew would search through each meal for any evidence of this hobby in their stew, though none of them had ever discovered so much as a fingernail. Second—and more important—no one faking death in the hopes of surviving the ordeal could ever have a finger cut off without screaming out in pain. Once exposed, each faker would be quickly finished off. It was this kind of attention to detail that had kept Gilcox and his ship an elusive mystery for so long.

The captain studied the Spanish ship. She was a merchant galley—fast, with three masts—but on this morning, she had been sailing slowly west, making herself easy prey. Gilcox knew that she had made this trip many times before, taking the same trade route as many other Spanish ships. They would transport gold and silver from the Americas to Spain, then take various goods to Africa before returning again to the Americas. This crew, like others they had encountered, had likely made this trip enough times that they had become sea-calloused to the dangers that still existed in these waters.

Gilcox had doubts about whether he and his crew should even bother seizing the ship. She was riding very low in the water toward the Americas and was unlikely to be carrying the cargo in which they were most interested. Her hold was filled with a human cargo, a mix of black African tribal people enslaved to work the mines and plantations of Spanish America. Yet something tempted him. The night was dark, the wind was right, and they were in perfect position to catch the Spaniards off their guard. From his wealth of experience, one could never know what surprise booty a ship might hold.

First Mate Blackbury took a half-step closer to Gilcox and leaned in to speak. It was not a subtle move, considering Blackbury's stature; everything about him was large. A broad-shouldered man, his dramatic face featured a big, bulldog nose with a crooked, broken bridge that protruded from below his massive forehead. His strong jaw had a distinct underbite and a chin that was so deeply cleft it looked as if he had been stuck with an ice pick. Even the toughest seadogs found his presence intimidating. Measuring well over six feet tall and weighing nearly twenty-five stone, his physical bearing was a perfect complement to Giddy's brilliant mind and horrifying features.

In a hushed tone, he whispered, "Cap'n, permission to speak in privacy?"

Gilcox enjoyed Blackbury's—and the entire crew's—respect for his command. They recognized his absolute authority as their captain, perhaps more than any other pirate crew on the seas. Other crews that he had been familiar with either practiced an awkward form of democracy or simply lived by survival of the fittest. There was no democracy within Gilcox's crew and no question about his rank as master and lord.

"Yes," the captain replied. "Mr. Blackbury, please speak openly."

As the captain and first mate turned their backs to the vengeful sport underway on deck, Blackbury said, "Cap'n, ya well know yer first mate and da crew ain't afraid of no man an' no fight." He paused to gauge his captain's reaction, unsure if he should continue.

An unnerving silence followed. Gilcox already knew where his first mate was going with this conversation. He wanted Blackbury to squirm a bit before he let him off the hook. Smirking, the captain finally broke the silence. "Yes, soldier, do proceed."

Blackbury flinched at Gilcox's reference to him as "soldier." This was intended to offend Blackbury, as it would any accomplished man of the sea. He used this verbal backhand to belittle his men and challenge them to better apply themselves. As Gilcox expected, it angered the first mate enough for him to press his point.

"Cap'n, dis ship's bad med'cine! The men don't care to mix wid dis cargo. I suggest we take what we got an' be off 'er!"

Gilcox knew that his crew had become aware of his plan to find a replacement vessel for his own beloved ship. He could sense that Blackbury and the crew were afraid that this sleek Spanish ship might just be the one.

The first mate continued, "The crew's been bringin' up Black Sam's name, sayin' they think it's da same evil what done Sam in when he took over da slavin' ship. It was the ship, *Whydah* what did him in! Dey don't want no part of dis one!"

Gilcox responded sternly, "Bellamy was a fool, and you're all fools if you believe in spirits. Black Sam was sloppy. He left evidence of his work everywhere—evidence and witnesses. Why, if that nor'easter hadn't sunk them off the Cape Cod, they would have been caught and hung like all the rest! A weakness for wine and women, a sudden change in weather, and poor seamanship are what undid that poor excuse for a sea captain."

"Well, sah, 'at might be true," Blackbury finished, "but da men's afraid ya fixin' to trade in *our* ship for 'er."

"*Our* ship?" Gilcox was incensed, and his gruesome face grew flush in anger. "She is *my* ship, upon which I deign the privilege to allow each of you to sail. Mr. Blackbury, I'm sure you do not share this same concern with the men but are merely performing your duty and relaying it. Therefore, whoever has spoken to you on this subject, please ask them to see me. I will be happy to *discuss* this matter with them directly."

Blackbury, recognizing that their conversation had just ended, immediately took a large step back and responded, "Aye, aye, Cap'n!"

Chapter Two

As the first mate stepped away, Gilcox decided he had to put an end to any of the crew's further discussion on the subject. He had, however, been experiencing the same eerie sensation as the rest of his crew. There was undoubtedly a unique and very ominous and evil presence upon this ship.

Gilcox had become a student of the great pirates before him and particularly valued anything that was written about them. He was a voracious reader and scoured any printed material that he could find. To him, the printed word was as valuable as the gold, silver, and jewels the pirates looted. Much had been written about Black Sam Bellamy and his ship.

The captain looked over his crew assembled on the back deck. He cleared his throat and in a loud voice began to share the story of Black Sam. "It was over thirty years ago that Black Sam captured the English slave ship *Whydah* in these waters. Bellamy and his pirate crew sailed north, with their destination being Richmond, Island of Maine."

At his first words, the pirates on deck halted their conversations and stopped what they were doing to listen.

"In April of 1717, Bellamy diverted their course to visit his mistress in Cape Cod. Black Sam and all but two of the 146 men on board the *Whydah* perished in a howling nor'easter. Many a superstitious pirate has since attributed the ship's demise to the slave trade she had once carried. "Don't be fools, soldiers. A ship is no more than wood and iron and tar and canvas. And these animals on this ship will soon be resting at the bottom of the sea. I alone will decide which ship we shall keep and which ship we'll scuttle. No more fool's talk of evil spirits. Let us finish our business and be off."

Gilcox glared at his first mate. He was not about to show his growing sense of foreboding about the Spanish ship to his men. He also was not ready to give up his beloved, yet increasingly recognized, ship. But that decision would be his alone.

He suddenly turned his attention to his bosun, Stroppy Newsome, who was leading a group of pirates from below deck. They were loud and excited, dragging topside what they had uncovered.

The captain shook his head in disgust. It was always his immediate reaction when he came into contact with his bosun. Gilcox had to remind himself that Newsome was an accomplished sailor who had proven effective at keeping the men in line. Yet the captain found the man's appearance and manner repulsive.

A short man, he was barrel-chested with thick arms and big hands. His face was almost completely hidden by both a heavy, long beard, which he had not trimmed since he had left the British navy, and a crumbling three-corner hat that, as best as Gilcox knew, had not been removed since that same time. All in all, he was a dirty man who had gleefully abandoned the personal hygiene disciplines of His Majesty's Service.

Stroppy had been thrown out of the navy in dishonor and without pension for continuously overstepping his bounds while doling out punishment to the errant sailors under his charge. There was no question that he was a capable seaman, but his constant grumbling and negative disposition made his superiors look for an excuse to be rid of him. When Giddy first met Stroppy on one of his voyages to the Far East, it was clear that he harbored a grudge against king and country upon which Giddy could capitalize.

The captain called out, "Mr. Newsome, what have you found? Please provide a full report."

"Yes, sah," Stroppy replied, dragging forward a man in chains. "What we's found among a few treashas and da provisions of salted meats, wine, gunpowda, muskets, and cutlery was dis hairy beast. He ain't one of da black animals below, but he sure is dark enough. What's does ya want us ta do wid 'im?"

Struggling to his feet against the weight of the chains was a very dark, short man, who was widely built and had coarse and curly black hair covering his entire body. He stood before Gilcox, badly beaten and in rags, squinting under the burning sunlight. He was clearly unsure as to whether or not this new turn of events would offer any improvement to his plight.

It occurred to Gilcox that the blinding sun must have made it impossible for this man to see Gilcox's frightful features clearly. It had saved the man from the involuntary look of repulsion toward the captain that had caused so many men to fall under his swift and bloody wrath.

"And you, you swarthy creature, if you speak from a common tongue, who are you, and have you been chained unjustly or justly?"

The man spoke in coarse, broken English. "I am Greek, named Niko Getsopolis. Captain, I shipwreck on Spanish soil and took to Madrid and told to sign on to ship for America. I say to you, 'unjust,' for these dirty Spanish took me on as ship hand, and I do my duty."

Gilcox knew that the Spanish fleet had indeed taken such heavy losses that they were desperate to sign on able-bodied seamen from any country that they did not consider their enemy.

"On the sea, they say I am pirate and beat me and chain me for no reason."

Gilcox didn't buy the man's story. "Are you indeed a pirate? Answer me straight, or I'll shave your neck right through those iron whiskers!"

"Captain, I am sailor of fortune with much time on Ivory Coast. I looking for transport to America."

Gilcox nodded to Newsome and, pointing with his saber to the irons, said, "Free him, and hand him your cutlass."

Newsome hesitated before grudgingly obeying his captain's order. With the chains clanking to the deck, Newsome held the sword out to the Greek. All was quiet as both the pirate and Spanish crew watched intently. The Greek eyed the weapon cautiously, likely wondering whether he should reject it or take it and fight for his life. Gilcox was enjoying watching this man in rags fearfully consider his options.

The Greek did not move for several seconds, seeming more like minutes, as he stared at the blade. However, just as Gilcox was about to give him further instruction, the Greek snatched the sword's handle faster than any buccaneer Gilcox had ever seen. In one swift pirouette, starting from his heels, the freed man drove the weapon a full blade depth into the neck of one of his captors. The Spanish bosun's eyes bulged, as only the sword handle protruded from the base of his neck. The attack happened so fast that the Greek's target had no time to react or make a sound. With a silent scream frozen on his lips, the Spaniard dropped lifelessly to the deck with a heavy thud.

Even the pirates were stunned. The Greek turned back to them, threw his hands in the air, and with a great smile, bowed with the flourish of an actor toward Gilcox. The buccaneers responded with a great and hearty cheer.

Giddy was entertained by the Greek's antics and caught himself almost revealing a rare smile. "Mr. Niko," he called out, "I suggest you take some clothes and weapons from your Spanish captors. You may join our crew, if you so desire."

The captain knew that there would be more tests for the Greek buccaneer to prove his worth, but for the time being, he was a crew member on the *Rogue Flattery*, the last of the great pirate ships.

~~~

One more pirate squarely in my debt. Gilcox surveyed his crew and reflected on his role as liberator. The Greek was not the first of his crew that he had freed from captured-ship irons. Many of those liberated mistakenly believed it had been an act of mercy. Gilcox experienced no such sentiment. He only understood that providing a second chance to desperate souls, regardless of how sinister or evil they might be, held value to him. As their liberator from certain doom, he benefited from a nearly blind devotion. He had learned the power of this redemption from his time in the church, which had provided a hiding place for him from the daily torment of his youth.

Gilcox's thoughts were interrupted by quartermaster Chauncy Cortlaroy, who was theatrically striding up to him. "Beggin' your pardon, sir," he trumpeted in a self-satisfied tone, "might I share a delightful thought with you?"

Knowing he had to humor the quartermaster on occasion, Gilcox responded, "Yes, Mr. Cortlaroy, what devious thought has come to your mind?"

"Captain, it would seem to me that we have a brilliant opportunity to have some further entertainment."

"Oh, really? And what form might that take, Cortlaroy?"

"Well, sir, in the form of living theater. A play about a reversal of fortune, as it were. Let us unchain the black animals and allow them a free hand to return favors to their captors!"

The thought of liberating the Africans and then turning the Spanish crew over to them had already crossed Gilcox's mind. The idea did not spring from an urge to see justice prevail but more for the same enjoyment that Cortlaroy likely sought by watching the ugly result of brutality repaid. The idea of the slaves' bloody retaliation against the Spaniards delighted the captain in the same way his piracy served as a rebellion against those who had oppressed him. It would also give him a chance to look over the cargo for slaves that might be of some value to him. But he knew his crew was anxious to leave, and they did not want to mingle with the ship's cargo.

The captain also knew that Cortlaroy was not a man to take "no" gracefully. Though he would argue his point with the best of politicians, with Gilcox it was different. The quartermaster would have to accept the captain's answer, though it would not sit well with him. It would be the crew that would have to endure his sulking anger, making everyone's life on the ship more miserable for it. It was a chance Gilcox would have to take.

"Yes," the captain responded, "the thought has already occurred to me, but the risk to me and my ship is simply not worth the folly. The longer we delay, the greater the chance the king's navy should appear on the horizon. Let us be done with this."

Chapter Three

Lashed together, the *Rogue Flattery* and the Spanish galley danced with the roll of the sea—one ship following the lead of the other, step by step. Captain Giddy Gilcox returned to his mistress ship and stood alone on the quarterdeck to watch over the transfer of the provisions and the small booty.

Most of the pirates, except for Blackbury and a half-dozen crew, had also already returned to the pirate ship to prepare for departure. The captain watched his first mate and boarding party struggle to open the heavy hatch to the Spanish ship's central hold.

As soon as they pulled the hatch open, the eerie, previously muffled cries from the cargo below escaped, sending a chill through Giddy's spine. He was surrounded by a cacophony like he had never heard before. Beyond the human wails and groans came the flapping of wings and shrieking howls from unknown beasts. The sound overwhelmed him, and he wondered, *Am I the only one hearing this madness?*

As he overcame the first wave of shock, he looked down at Blackbury. As hard and tough as any buccaneer Gilcox had ever encountered, Blackbury had stepped back from the din and hunched down as though he were being threatened by a loaded flintlock. Surveying his crew, Gilcox saw each of his men step back in horror from the sound. Some ducked away, while others grabbed for their weapons. Blackbury snuck a look at his captain.

To keep up appearances, Giddy would not acknowledge what he was experiencing and did not respond to his first mate's silent question. "Send the Spaniards below and return to the ship, Mr. Blackbury."

Blackbury straightened up, pulled out his cutlass, and shouted to the rest of the boarding party, "All right, let's show dese Spanish their new accommodations!"

He stabbed at the first Spanish sailor, forcing him to drop into the hold. The rest of the boarding party followed suit, stabbing and pushing the Spaniards toward the opening to a drop of some twelve feet. The captured sailors clutched at each other in fear, causing them to topple over the twelve-foot drop, one by one, like links of a big sea chain. The Spaniards' cries of pain and horror swelled with those of the Africans as they landed on top of their former cargo. Those at the bottom were likely to be crushed to death.

Watching others endure pain and suffering would normally be a source of great entertainment for the pirates, but Gilcox noticed that many of them were cringing and looking away, as if experiencing the horror themselves. This brutality was nothing new to these pirates. These men, who had committed some of the cruelest and most brutal crimes against humanity, were now trembling at the sounds of horror coming from below the Spanish ship's deck.

Gilcox turned away, feigning disinterest. Was this indeed some evil spirit they had had the bad fortune to stumble upon? Why was it such a struggle for him and his crew?

At the sound of the heavy hatch slamming shut, Gilcox turned back to Blackbury. "Mr. Blackbury, return to the ship, cut the lines, and push off. Let us be finished with this business."

Blackbury and the boarding party leapt back aboard the *Rogue Flattery*. The two ships were untied, and the pirates eagerly pushed off from the Spanish galley.

~~~

As the ship drifted away, Stroppy Newsome called out, "Next gunner forward!"

The crew simultaneously stepped back from a cannon located on the starboard rail, and one man stepped forward. "Aye, 'at would be me, Stroppy," the man said nervously.

Newsome smiled and said, "Tinsdale, is it? I'll enjoy takin' da cat-o-nine ta ya back. Give it a go, ya poor sod."

Tinsdale went to the cannon and prepared the charge.

The Greek moved next to Newsome, who stood just below Gilcox. Giddy listened in on their conversation. The Greek asked, "Why you want to sink that ship? She worth much. What is this captain doing?"

Newsome glared at the Greek. "Ya better learn quick wid dis cap'n and crew. Cap'n Gilcox don't want ta leave no clues. Each sailor is given a turn ta take one shot ta scuttle da ships we capture. He's either scourged fa failure or rewarded wid gold fa success. Gilcox demands dat any ship sunk must go under evenly—water rising equally up port, starboard, bow, and stern, wid da very tip of da main mast being da last point ta drop below da surface."

The Greek shook his head. "What is purpose of this? It is impossible."

"Well, let me tell ya, ya muddy-mouth animal. I don't like ya, and I don't like da way ya talk. If it was up ta me, ya'd be trapped wid da rest of those animals preparing ta meet Davy Jones. But da cap'n made ya crew, and dis crew gots a couple o' teachers. Der names are Mistah Fear and Mistah Pain. Dese schoolmasters will teach ya how ta do things like da way da cap'n wants 'em done."

Stroppy paused but then felt the need to emphasize his point. "Cap'n wants certain things done like he wants 'em. Ya don't asks no questions. Ya just do it. Scuttling ships is one of dose things. I swears da only thing 'at touches Gilcox's cold heart is seeing a sinking ship's bow or stern lift out of da water. Da cap'n turns into a bloody demon, and ya doesn't want ta be on da receivin' end of his unearthly wrath."

It was true; there was nothing that caused Giddy Gilcox to become more emotional than the sight of a great ship raising its bow or stern up out of the water and revealing her wound like a large, dying mammal to be swallowed by the sea. He hated the feeling, and his only relief for it was violence.

The ship had fallen quiet, and all attention turned to the gunner. Visibly nervous, Tinsdale took aim and lit the fuse. With a great explosion, the ball burst open a large hole at the galley's waterline. Water immediately gushed in and dispersed throughout, filling the ship. She rocked port to starboard and bow to stern, but then settled steadily— amongst the cries of the Spaniards and the African cargo—as the great vessel began to slowly submerge.

~~~

Blackbury joined his captain, and the two silently watched from the quarterdeck.

The first mate broke the silence. "One more Spanish ship deliva'd ta a wat'ry grave for king an' country."

"Yes, indeed," Gilcox solemnly answered.

There was a time when his countrymen took pride in the pirate's privateering successes of sinking ship after ship of the once-great Spanish treasure fleet, though the pirate rogues never had any true loyalty to the crown.

The names of the famous pirate captains who had come before him flashed in Gilcox's mind—Kidd, Vaine, Morgan, Bellamy, and Blackbeard. He had held a grudging respect for them, but when they started plundering the English colonies and the king's own ships, he felt they became too interested in making names for themselves.

The pirate captain wondered aloud, "If those who came before us hadn't been so greedy and so bloody sloppy, we might not have had to take such precautions as we do today." He stared at the sinking ship. "Such a waste of so fine a vessel. Yet the king had no choice but to put an end to those fools. We pay the price for it today."

For over twenty years, Horacio "Giddy" Gilcox, the son of a ship-builder and outfitter, had plied his pirate trade. Unlike those other, inept pirate captains, he was a brilliant sailor who commanded a unique respect and devotion to duty from his crew. His ability to capture, plunder, and sink ship after ship was unparalleled. Giddy's fearless confidence grew from his proven ability to outwit any adversary.

He and his crew of salty dogs quietly watched the Spanish ship submerge. Giddy knew that these simple-minded buccaneers needed a sharp mind to do the thinking for them, and for his money, there was unquestionably none keener than his own.

Blackbury looked away from the sinking ship and over to his captain. "No, dem pirates made a name fa demselves awright. Dey wasn't da smartest ship cap'ns, but dey sure wasn't afraid a nothin' on earth, nor heaven nor hell. No, sir."

"Now keep in mind, Mr. Blackbury," Gilcox said sternly, "what makes us different from all those who went before us—our ability to stay in the watery shadows. This is the greatest reason for our success."

While Blackbeard and the other pirates had paraded about shame-lessly, flying their own flags and flaunting their exploits to the Crown's embarrassment, Gilcox and his men quietly and efficiently went about their business, leaving few traces. Ships they pirated and scuttled were assumed lost to stormy seas or other pirates.

Even their anchorage, Albatross Island, provided them with not only a hidden port but, because of its inhabitants' notoriety for luring ships into their coast to be shipwrecked and then plundered, also provided them with a clever cover.

Gilcox continued, "The other pirates were too damn greedy and enjoyed their notoriety too much. It led them all—each and every one of them—to finish their piracy with a dangle at the end of a rope…or something even worse."

Blackbury weighed his words cautiously, aware that he was dancing along the edge of frank conversation and insubordination. "Even wid all dese precautions we've taken, I'm afraid da evidence of our existence is beginning ta surface like the loose debris of dat dere ship sinking afore us. All it takes is an unguarded tongue 'ere or a survivah dere. We certainly know dey's on ta us. I'm afraid we gots dere attention. Word is dat da papers back in England are printin' articles 'bout ya, Cap'n."

Giddy had come across several such articles, which he had kept from his men. Though he espoused notoriety as deplorable, he secretly relished the recognition that he was certain he deserved. In much the same way as his predecessors, he wanted the world to know of his brilliance.

One of his most treasured possessions was a recent scrap from an English newspaper. The article contained doggerel that Giddy himself had since heard sailors and landlubbers alike recite.

A scurvy dog, this Giddy Gilcox
While others drink rum, he prefers his gin
The look from his twisted face
Enough to make one feel worms crawl up their skin
And don't be disarmed by his jolly name
For if so unfortunate as to see Giddy grin
It's only when he's about to taste blood
And do some poor soul in!

That same article spoke of a royal order to put an end to the colonial piracy and to roust Giddy and his crew. It mentioned a young and aspiring British commander, Leslie Christian, who received orders bearing His Majesty's seal. As far as Giddy knew, Christian's ship, the HMS *Sovereign,* was hunting him down at this very moment. This was of little concern to Giddy, for he was confident he could outwit any officer in the king's navy.

For now, his real concern focused on the strange, unsettling feeling that seemed to have followed them from the Spanish ship back to the *Rogue Flattery*. He felt some relief when the waters crested over the main deck to silence the wretched cries of the cargo. He hoped that once this cursed ship and its cargo disappeared below the water's surface, the haunting feeling would be taken with it.

Giddy and the crew were silent as the tall masts swiftly and quietly vanished, leaving a circle of floating debris as a grave marker. The buccaneers stood by quietly as their ship rocked to the wake left by the sunken craft, staring at the spot that a moment before had been occupied by the sleek Spanish vessel.

Giddy took a deep breath and exhaled. Rubbing his hands together, he felt with mild surprise the clammy sweat in his palms. There was no doubt he was relieved that the ship was gone. He wondered if the crew felt the same relief sweep over them. Giddy decided he and his pirates had actually done a good deed in sending the evil spirit aboard the ship to a watery grave.

The buccaneers had all solemnly—almost reverently—watched the Spanish ship disappear to her final rest at the bottom of the sea, and it occurred to Giddy that for this pirate crew, watching a ship buried at sea was as close to a remorseful funeral service as they would ever attend.

The silence aboard ship was suddenly broken with Bosun Stroppy Newsome's call to quarters. He cracked his leather club on the cap rail, and the crew immediately scrambled as he hollered, "Ta ya stations, ya no-good landlubbers! Ya're as worthless as seagull spray! Let's put some distance betwixt us and that foul Spanish odor we just sent ta hell!"

Gilcox shook his head in disgust at the filthy bosun, but he couldn't help but agree with his sentiment.

Chapter Four

The crystal-clear turquoise water lapped onto the white-sand beach as palm trees swayed in the balmy breeze of Albatross Island. Giddy Gilcox took off his plumed hat to wipe the sweat from his brow. He closed his eyes and lifted his face to feel the breeze course through the sparse growth of hair. Turning in the opposite direction, he opened his eyes, noting the stark contrast to the island view off on the opposite shore. In the distance lay a wooden carcass, decaying between the waves and the rocks. Like flies circling over a rotting fish, seagulls swarmed and dove at the crustaceans crawling about the ship's exposed bowels.

After landing and dismissing the crew, Gilcox set off for the wreck with Blackbury and Niko, the Greek, to determine if anything further could be salvaged. Giddy judged the Greek to be both intelligent and enterprising. These qualities in a crew member could prove troubling to a pirate captain, but Gilcox had other plans for his newest recruit.

"What happened to this ship?" Niko asked.

Blackbury answered with an air of condescension. "This ship, like others, was lured onto da hidden reefs offshore weeks ago by da lanterns of our island natives. Dey use da lanterns ta make 'em appear as ships' lights, causing other ship captains ta think da waters are navigable. And here dey ends up."

Albatross Island was a small, yet foreboding island of only some twenty miles in circumference. Much of its coast was a long, shallow sandbar with large reefs and breakers only exposed at low tide. Unlike all other islands in the Caribbean, Albatross not only had the coral but also large rocky shoals, some as far as two thousand of the king's feet from the visible shore. This in itself gave many a ship's captain cause for a wide berth around the island.

For those brave souls who ever even attempted a landing, upon reaching the beach and facing her impenetrable forest and high, steep cliffs, all climbed back in their longboats, never to return.

With the island's proximity to two other islands that had well-known ports servicing all the shipping through the area, there really was no reason for anyone to trouble with Albatross. Add to all that, a healthy superstition of the natives, fueled by rumors of black magic and cannibalism, and no ship with knowledge of the Caribbean seas ever bothered with Albatross Island.

"Captain, you have done much good for you and this crew. Why you come to this place? Why this island not scare you, too?"

Giddy cringed at the Greek's coarse use of English. Though the captain liked his privacy, he occasionally needed someone with whom to exercise his mind. The Greek was new blood, and Gilcox was gauging whether the Greek might provide him with some intellectual entertainment. At the moment, though, he was having a hard time getting beyond his thick accent.

"Well, indeed, Mr. Niko, you'll find that this captain will not tolerate fear in himself or any of his crew. The keenest of minds would quickly surmise that all of the reasons why others avoid the island are precisely why it should be the choice as our hideaway."

The Greek took the opportunity to flatter Gilcox. "Captain, you have strong mind. Who could be match for you?"

Giddy caught himself almost falling for the Greek's flattery. "Yes, but sometimes intelligence comes in the form of fortune and perseverance. We took our time and incurred great risk until we uncovered this very fine port, now the exclusive domain of the *Rogue Flattery*."

Gilcox had had enough of this conversation. As he surveyed the wreck, his thoughts turned back to the Spanish slave ship, and he felt that queer sensation once again. He abruptly stopped talking and walked off toward the wreck.

Even though he was disappointed that the Greek would not provide him with the intellectual stimulation for which he had hoped, it was obvious that Niko was a troublemaker, a fact that would work right into Gilcox's plans. He would allow the Greek to be drawn in as one of the crew, assured that there would be enough fear and respect for his captain that the Greek would bide his time before stirring up the crew to mutiny. The captain would wait for an obvious opportunity that only he, himself, could provide.

~~~

Blackbury looked over at his captain. "He's bloody brilliant, but I sometimes wonder if he ain't somefin even more den a man. I be warnin' ya now, Mistah Niko, don't be crossing dis cap'n."

"Ohhi, ohhi," the Greek responded, hoping it was loud enough that Gilcox could hear. "No, no. This great captain save me from Spanish devils. I do nothing bad. I only please this captain. He can trust Niko as good sailor!" The Greek scratched his chin and, in a softer voice, inquired, "Do the men like this place? I don't think I like these native peoples."

Blackbury sighed with resignation and quietly answered, "It is our home."

For the pirates, Albatross Island was their home. All except the captain had native wives. The natives viewed Gilcox with awe—to them, he was some form of a god, a reincarnation of a native spirit worshiped on the island for years. They served his every wish out of fear, but he also was good to them. Although it bothered his crew, he shared much of the stolen provisions the pirates brought back to the island.

Gilcox's sharing with the natives was not out of feelings of love or generosity but because he knew it created a blend of fear and gratitude that gave him greater control over them. He would encourage the natives to lure in ships, like the wreck on the beach. If any sailors survived the wreck, they'd be killed and the ship stripped of anything that was worth anything. After the rocks and coral would sufficiently break up the ship, the ship timbers would be salvaged to build the cabins, docks, and stockades back in their village.

One thing for which Giddy Gilcox would pay handsomely was the retrieval of any kind of written materials. Before the pirates arrived on the island, this material would go straight down to the coral. Now, the natives gathered it up—maps, ship logs, parchments—and immediately delivered it to Gilcox. His satisfaction with the prize gave the natives a feeling that something good would happen to them, whether in this life or the next.

Chapter Five

Giddy Gilcox stood over the desk in his cabin, looking at his calendar. He marked a large X over the previous day, one more in a long series of X's. As he pondered what would come next for the pirates, he felt a restless anxiety stirring within him. It was now two weeks since the sinking of the Spanish ship, and his pirate crew was becoming bored and restless on their island home. Suddenly, a strong gust of wind entered the window and blew the papers from his desk. He stepped outside his hut and recognized the stirring winds of a coming storm.

Blackbury had also stepped out of his hut next door to gauge the weather. "Mr. Blackbury," Gilcox called out, "it appears that we are in for a blow. Have the *Rogue Flattery* battened down, and let us retreat to the safety of the island caves."

Blackbury called back, "Aye, aye, Cap'n!"

~~~

Twenty-four hours later, Giddy Gilcox stepped out from the caves to verify that the storm was subsiding. The men drifted from the caves and stood milling about as they waited for the "all clear" from their captain.

Just as he was about to signal his men to return to the village, Giddy noticed a native man excitedly running up to the caves. Stroppy Newsome intercepted the native and listened at length to the agitated man, while Gilcox waited impatiently for his bosun's report.

"Beggin' ya pardon, sah," Stroppy said as he approached his captain, "but da natives has a bit of news for ya."

"Yes, Mr. Newsome," said the captain coolly, "and your report is…?"

Stroppy carefully chose his words. "It appears dat der is quite a bit of debris in da lagoon, but our cabins and da *Rogue Flattery* has survived pretty good."

Gilcox responded, "Very well. The men and their wives shall return to the lagoon village and begin the cleanup. But the native seemed very excited, Mr. Stroppy. Did he have any other news for us?"

Stroppy took a gulp and came closer so that only the captain could hear. "Yes, indeed, sah. He reported a large ship was listin' in da waters off da far breakers ta da nor'east of da island."

There was something about Stroppy Newsome's manner that irritated the captain. He wondered why the bosun had held back this important information. *How much longer can I put up with him?* The captain controlled his anger and said, "Go and take a large party of natives to comb the beaches, then board the wreck. Don't leave anyone alive. Report back to me as soon as you're through."

Stroppy exhaled and answered, "Aye, aye, Cap'n," before returning to the native messenger and giving the signal to attack the mystery ship.

A large group of natives had now gathered with the one who'd brought the report. As though a starting pistol for a grand footrace had just been fired, the natives all bolted through the forest to their canoes. Gilcox watched with disgust as Stroppy Newsome slowly plodded through the forest behind them.

~~~

Stroppy Newsome lagged far behind the natives. When he finally reached the beach, they were already at work, pulling the loose debris inland, including barrels, tackle, rope, sail, and splintered wood. Among the haul were eight bodies. One appeared to be the captain, judging by the lace on his shirt and the look of his clothes.

One of the natives came out of the woods and excitedly waved to the others, motioning them to quietly follow him back into the woods. A group of six headed off into the brush.

Stroppy wondered what they were after. He came slowly up the beach, looking over the materials and the dead men scattered about. One of the natives waved him into the brush and signaled for him to be quiet. There were tracks that led to four survivors who had dragged themselves off the beach and huddled together for comfort. The islanders quietly approached the shipwrecked men, undetected, as Stroppy made his way closer to give them instructions.

Stroppy was angry with himself. He had made a mistake by holding back the information on the new wreck from Gilcox, and he knew the captain was angry. He survived the captain's wrath then, but would he pay for it later? He had greedily tried to keep the information to himself, wanting to check on the wreck to get first take on what was found. Now he had to go with the natives, who would report on everything to their "god" Gilcox. Stroppy hated working with the natives. With the pirates, he could whip and beat the men, but he could not touch the natives—Gilcox would not allow it.

The pirate came quietly through the brush and found the natives crouching and listening to the men talking. Stroppy stopped and listened, too.

It was a cool morning following the tempest, and the sailors were shivering from exposure. Their teeth chattered not only due to the elements but probably in fear. The men spoke in anxious whispers about being stranded on the cursed island, Albatross, and being discovered by the native cannibals.

Stroppy listened in and found himself relating to these men in their condition. Their shivering and fear struck a chord with him and brought to mind his own terrible recurring nightmare: As a child, Stroppy Newsome was beaten regularly by his father. As an adult, he felt a need to extend the same level of abuse, particularly to those who were smaller and less capable of defending themselves.

The terrible dream repeated a scene of his lying in a small open boat, sore and bruised, being tossed about by a wild storm. He was always completely soaked and shivering, but the water was strangely warm. The lightning was strong and bright and each raindrop huge, hitting him hard, like fists. The last lightning bolt cracked the sky open with a blinding flash that then revealed an image of his father with his huge fist reared back. His fist started forward and, like a massive meteor, streaked down straight for Stroppy.

Stroppy was always jolted awake, screaming, soaked in sweat and urine, as the punch struck and created the lightning flash of being hit squarely in the eye. His biggest concern after one of his nightmares, though, was how long he had been screaming and who might have heard. Certainly, none of the crew would address it. They did all seem to stay clear of Stroppy the following day, not only in fear of his vengeful temper, undoubtedly, but also because of his horrible stench.

Stroppy signaled to the natives to silently move in on the four men. Suddenly, the survivors found themselves surrounded by natives with spears and clubs. The frightened men pulled together in a circle, with their backs against one another and their hands pressed together as they began pleading for their lives.

Stroppy broke through the ring of natives. He could see their hope of salvation rise when they saw a white man with a long beard amongst the natives. Stroppy flashed a sinister smile. "Good day, boys. You men serve our king under the Union Jack?"

"Yes, yes, we are Englishmen," one of the men answered through chattering teeth. "Blimey, it's bloody good ta see a countryman."

Stroppy's smile disappeared. He turned to the natives, signaled them by drawing his thumb across his throat, and disappeared back to the beach. As Stroppy walked away, he could hear the last man blurt out, "Gawd save our kang!" as a club came down with a thud on his skull. Silence followed.

Stroppy smiled and shook his head. *A lot ya bloody king has done for ya.*

At the beach, the natives readied a canoe to ferry Stroppy out to the sinking ship. As they approached, he could see the ship was in a precarious position. In a few hours, the ebbing tide would take her down. Stroppy knew that if there was anything of value on board, they would have to move quickly to retrieve it.

Once on board the ship, Stroppy went through the captain's quarters but found it deserted, with few valuables. The natives feverishly searched for the printed materials—what they thought of as "funny leaves" bound together and covered with shapes like little bugs. This was the strange treasure Gilcox coveted so dearly. However, there was little to be found on this ship but a diary, the ship's maps, and the log.

The fastest young native runner was chosen to take the strange treasure to Gilcox. This was always a great honor, filled with excitement and fear for the natives as they wondered if the prize would please him.

Stroppy was disappointed when he found only a few coins and the captain's cutlery. Aside from the ship provisions and arms, he knew Gilcox would be disappointed, too. Before leaving the ship, Stroppy took a quick look into the cargo hold to see what Davey Jones would soon be devouring. Stroppy's eyes widened, and he knew the rest of the pirates would be overjoyed. The vast cargo hold, slowly filling with seawater, contained barrel upon barrel of aged rum.

Chapter Six

Back in his cabin, the pirate captain reviewed a map with Blackbury of the northeastern American seaboard. Motion outside the window caught the captain's eye. Looking up, he saw a young native boy sprinting through the village toward the cabin, carrying a burlap pouch.

"Well, well," Giddy muttered. "It looks like the natives have retrieved some of my favorite treasure."

Blackbury looked up, noticing the size of the pouch. "Well, I'm afraid it looks to be a small treasure, Cap'n."

The boy stopped at the porch in front of the entrance to the captain's cabin, while the two men watched through the open door. As the boy struggled to catch his breath, he placed the bag at the door, stepped back off the porch, and knelt to tap on the wood with the tips of his fingers. The boy kept his head down, and Giddy could see his body trembling.

The captain came to the door, followed by Blackbury. The boy kept his head down and stared at Gilcox's feet, clearly afraid to gaze upon this deity. After a moment, though, he overcame his fear to steal a quick glance at the great Gilcox.

When the boy looked up, Giddy caught a glimpse of the child's face. There was no sign of fear in the boy's eyes. Gilcox had seen him before—he remembered the boy for his disfigured face. A birth defect had left the boy with a cleft upper lip and mangled nose. Each time he saw the boy, it made Gilcox think back to his own childhood.

As a young child, before the onset of his illness, Giddy's parents had taken such pride in his handsome features and happy disposition. His joyous smile, contagious laugh, and pleasant demeanor gave his father great delight when he returned home at the end of a day's work. Upon entering the house, his father would declare, "And how is my giddy little one today?" From there, his nickname took root.

But disease struck Giddy while he was still young. Happy little Giddy Gilcox turned quickly into a creature from which even his parents had difficulty hiding their repulsion. His ultimate degradation came when his parents could no longer endure the embarrassment and required Giddy to don a cloth mask that completely covered his head when out in public. The sudden rejection and the abuse he bore over the years drove him to a life of seclusion and, ultimately, to violence. His intelligence, his cold, calculating heart, his keenness for violence, and a love of ships naturally found a perfect union in piracy.

Giddy stood there, lost in the painful memories of his childhood. Blackbury glanced at Giddy and nodded knowingly, then reached down, picked up the bag, and handed it to his captain. Giddy took the bag and was drawn back to the present. He jostled the sack disappointedly. With a harsh grunt, he turned back to go into his cabin.

Before he went through the door, he paused and, feeling a sense of compassion for the disfigured boy, extended his highest words of praise to the native. "Well done, ye fine idiot! Away with ye!"

He waved to his first mate to pay the boy in silver chain and then entered the cabin. The slam of the door jolted the boy, and he jumped up. Giddy turned back and, through his window, saw the boy running off into the jungle. He felt a twinge of remorse; Giddy somehow knew the boy ran in fear that he had failed and with that failure, he would suffer eternal consequences. No token gift would ever overcome that.

It was something to which Giddy could strangely relate in his own life.

Giddy Gilcox would never admit it, but no matter how much the pirate stole and plundered, it never seemed to be enough. There was always an empty feeling; something that seemed missing. His mind went back again to the Spanish slave ship. The ship had continued to haunt him. He wondered if there was some connection between his past and the evil he had felt upon that galley.

Once again, he shook off these feelings and spilled the contents of the bag onto the table. Searching through the written materials would take his mind off such foolish thoughts.

~~~

Sachumjuia sat on the barge, watching the pirates work as hard as he had ever seen them work. Feverishly, they brought kegs of rum up from the ship, onto a raft, and from the raft to the barge tethered by a long thick rope to the sinking ship. The pirates repeated this effort over and over. He had supervised the pirates in setting up the rope rigging that extended from the ship to the barge. The raft moved back and forth, transporting the ship cargo to the barge. When they were done, the barge would be sailed into the lagoon. He would not help. There was no value in this drink to him. It did not quench his thirst; it only served to make him and the others stupid.

When word of the rum had gotten out amongst the pirates, they dropped their clearing efforts at the lagoon to retrieve the liquid treasure. They knew it wouldn't be long before the tide lifted the great ship off the rocks and dragged her out to the ocean deep to deposit her booty forever.

The large and powerful Mohegan Indian brave-turned-pirate knew the captain restricted how much rum they had on hand and how much rum was taken from the ships they pillaged. His captain would claim he did not want to weigh his stealthy craft down, but the Indian knew the real problem lay in the difficulty of captaining a drunken crew. At the moment, though, Gilcox was deeply into the quiet seclusion he required as he painstakingly studied the ship documents. The crew was taking full advantage of the distraction. They were free to salvage their rum without any limit but that which the tide allowed.

By evening, the perilous work had earned the pirates a third of the ship's cargo before she started to break up on the rocks. Sachumjuia watched as they readied to shove off, wondering if any of them would realize their failure.

Captain Gilcox always required the nameplate from every plundered ship. If the captain realized they'd worked all day collecting rum and left her name to the coral, there would be bloodshed. He could take it out on any one of them. The waves were mounting, and the ship was crying out as timbers bent and twisted. Soon, she'd break apart and slip away.

Sachumjuia shook his head as he watched the crew and thought, *These are men with simple minds.*

One of the pirates suddenly realized their failure and blurted out to the others, "Bloody hell! We've forgotten her name! Someone's got to get it!"

Anxiously, the pirates looked at one another in hopes that another would volunteer. They all then turned their faces to the stoic Indian as the obvious choice.

Sachumjuia sat with his legs crossed, mulling over whether he should bother to save them from their own stupidity. Salvaging rum for drunken pirates was decidedly not his purpose in life. He had always been driven by a keen sense of destiny, and yet nothing seemed to satisfy this yearning within him. He thought of where he had come from as the pirates begged him to retrieve the nameplate.

He was a brave from the Mohegan wolf clan of Quinnetucket. Sachumjuia had decided that the broken arrow peace established with the English by the sachem Chief Uncas—and continued by his sachem sons—had failed. Though the brave had fought alongside the English, he could no longer bear to see the pale invaders steadily steal away

Maheganeak land. He was captured while staging a single-handed bloody assault on British colonists.

He had hoped his violent rebellion would stir his brothers to rise up, but the long-standing peace had softened them and none would follow. After his capture and while en route to Boston, he escaped from the British prison ship into the Block Island Sound. He was then spotted in the water and picked up by a slave ship headed from Newport to the Southern colonies. The slave ship added him to its cargo of black slaves without knowing they had a notoriously murderous Mohegan in their grasp.

Sachumjuia exploited the careless crew, and by his enormous strength, stealth, and savagery, he was able to slay the entire crew and seize control of the slave ship. Neither he nor any of the slaves on board could sail the ship, so they drifted until a privateer came upon her. Realizing that something was amiss, the privateers sent a volley of cannonballs meant to stun those on board the slave ship. One of the shots caused more damage than was intended, and the ship quickly sank. Only Sachumjuia could swim; the rest of the slaves drowned. Picked out of the water, he was set in chains once again until the pirate captain Giddy Gilcox and his crew plundered the privateer ship the following week.

The pirate captain's keen eye recognized the value in Sachumjuia and took him on as a member of his crew. No chains were required, and Sachumjuia felt freer than he had ever felt in his life. Never before had this brave been treated anything like an equal with the white man. He would follow this demon pirate chief almost anywhere and do whatever he asked. His athletic prowess to run, jump, swim, track, hunt, fish, and fight was like none that the pirates had ever seen. His skills were beyond any of the other crew, and Captain Gilcox took full advantage of him.

As the pirates stared at Sachumjuia, he picked up his hatchet and tucked it into his belt without a word. From the raft, he climbed hand over hand across the rope to the ship. Just as he stepped on board, she started steadily moving out and down to the coral.

The pirates had to chop the rope to cut the barge loose from the sinking ship so as not to be pulled down with her. The bowsprit was sticking almost straight out of the water as Sachumjuia grabbed hold and, while straddling the bow, began furiously chopping away at her nameplate.

He overheard one of the pirates yell, "Blimey, it looks like a great swordfish done got hold of 'is leg and 'e's choppin' away, trying to free 'isself. He's goin' down!"

As Sachumjuia hacked at the wood at the nameplate, the idea of battling a great fish gave him the sense of purpose and the challenge he always sought. This work was no longer about just retrieving a piece of wood but had become an epic struggle between man and beast.

The pirates seemed to sense the same battle; he could hear them cheering him on as he fought against the ship-turned-swordfish.

The Mohegan felt the waters rising up over his legs, and he chopped away with greater effort to kill the beast. Locked in battle, the two began to submerge. Sachumjuia's raised hatchet and the great sword of the bowsprit were the last to be seen as both slid beneath the water's surface.

~~~

The pirates on the raft stopped cheering. The ship had taken the Indian down with it. As the minutes passed, another pirate wondered aloud, "I do believe our Indian has done lost da battle ta dat great swordfish. Ain't no way nobody kin stay under dis long."

"Da pull of the ship an' da undertow must 'ave grabbed hold of da Indian."

The pirates continued to stare at the spot in disbelief. Suddenly, floating in the water before them was the ship breastplate, reading *Cane's Burden.*

The first pirate said, "Blimey, 'e's done it. But what in hell 'as 'appened to 'im?"

They continued to search the water for any sight of the Indian, but there was no sign. When they turned to pull the barge back to shore, they were startled to see the dripping-wet Sachumjuia sitting there, cross-legged, just as he had been when they had first requested his services.

Chapter Seven

Giddy stayed cloistered in his cabin while poring over his precious materials from the shipwreck. He had always been most comfortable retreating to a world that could provide intellectual stimulation. He started with the maps, scouring them inch by inch for anything that he had not seen charted before. Obviously, he was most interested in those charts covering the Caribbean seas. He noticed, with some satisfaction, that the shipping lanes near Albatross now provided for a wider berth around the island.

But what's this? His blood stopped. He retrieved his reading glass to have a closer look. There appeared to be an ink mark on the centimeter-long depiction of the island. It was marked in blue, not the customary black. Even more disconcerting was that it was placed roughly where the opening of the lagoon would be. Hurriedly, he scanned the edges of the map, where he found one word, also written in blue ink: *VANISHED*.

Giddy's pulse began to quicken as he swiped the maps from his desk with one arm and grabbed the ship's log with the other. The question was, when had the mark been made? Was it old or new? He concluded that if it were more than two weeks old and the captain had reported anything, the navy would have been upon him by now. He went back two weeks in the log and started reading forward. It was clear that at that time, this ship had been sailing on a course heading northwest to Jamaica. The entry on the fifth day indicated that they were then in the vicinity of the island. Giddy stopped to realize that this was the same day the *Rogue Flattery* had last returned to port.

Log date: 21 September, 1749, ___ latitude, ___ longitude.

We are a day's delay from our scheduled arrival, but today held blue sky and a strong wind off our stern. Crew was jumpy as we passed to the east of Albatross. Most of the men will not even set their gaze upon it. Though it slowed us further, we gave her much leeway. I do jot down one item of note: Not certain it was the strong sun in my eyes or some black magic for which the island is well noted, but if my eyes deceived me, they never have before. Surely, I saw a ship that, at first, seemed so close to the island as to have been beached but upright. Her sails were down, and the island seemed to be swallowing her whole! As I retrieved my spyglass and put it up to my eye, the ship was gone! Immediately, I gave orders to come about and sail in a more easterly direction.

No one else on the ship can confirm this sighting. It is a fearful thought that an island can have such power. I wonder how close a ship might stray to Albatross before falling within her grasp.

Giddy stopped to consider who was on watch at the time they arrived at the island. Clearly, he had conveyed the seriousness of being spotted while entering the lagoon. He swore that someone would pay a painful price for this stupidity. Then again, it appeared that the sighting had only added to the mystique and fear of the island. Feeling less anxious, he continued reading at a more leisurely pace. An entry made in the log two days later made him take notice.

Log date 23 September, 1749, ___ latitude, ___ longitude.

The wind and currents are favorable with clear skies. Another delay beset us as a castaway was spotted off our starboard bow. Lowering a boat, we fished the sailor from the sea. It was plain to see he had been drifting for several days and was in poor condition, being out of his mind with scurvy. He had at some point suffered a severe blow to the head, a clean stab wound to the side and, strangest of all, the pointer finger on his right hand was missing. Once on board the ship, his mutterings were thought to be Spanish. This was confirmed when, at one point, he sat bolt upright and screamed, "*El diablo!*" ("the devil"). I'm quite certain the poor wretch will not survive many days longer.

The haunting terror I see in this man's eyes I cannot help but believe has some connection to the cursed island Albatross we passed not two days ago. The crew, having their own suspicions, argued amongst themselves and went to the first mate, beseeching him to convince me that we should return the castaway to the sea. I addressed the crew directly and denied their request on the grounds of Christian moral suasion and the seamen's code of conduct. I await the morning to gauge their response.

Log date 23 September, 1749, evening

This evening, the Spaniard succumbed to his injuries and was pronounced dead. Regretfully, I say all on board, including this captain, were relieved. Upon a hasty burial service, he was then returned to the sea.

Gilcox hurriedly read on to find that the captain, upon reaching his destination of Jamaica, requested and was granted an audience with the governor. The governor, being most interested, asked the captain to relay this information directly to Lieutenant Commander Leslie Christian, now stationed in Jamaica. The captain wrote that Christian was keenly interested, asking many questions about the island and the mysterious ship that had vanished within it.

Giddy had become aware of the Royal Navy captain after his men found notices posted around the major ports, indicating that the Royal Navy was soliciting information about Giddy's whereabouts. Lieutenant Commander Leslie Christian of His Majesty's Royal Navy appeared determined to make his mark with the Crown. *How capable an adversary is this naval officer?* Giddy wondered. If Christian were overly anxious, Giddy reasoned, he probably would have mobilized quickly and might be approaching the island at any moment. If that were true, he would be ill-prepared to engage the pirates on land. If he had recruited a shore party of marines, that likely would have taken time, for few would jump at the chance to land on Albatross.

Gilcox determined that, either way, their home port was now useless to them. If the pirates succeeded in defending the island against Christian, there only would be more navy to follow. Besides, they were pirates; if there was fighting to do, Gilcox would take his chances upon the *Rogue Flattery*! Best to make haste to avoid being bottled up while exiting the narrow channel from the lagoon.

The captain called First Mate Blackbury, Bosun Newsome, and Quartermaster Cortlaroy to his cabin. When the last had closed the cabin door behind him, Gilcox bellowed, "Soldiers, we have been discovered!"

The three pirates looked at each other with surprise. Blackbury cautiously asked, "Cap'n, are ya certain of dis?"

Giddy ignored the question. "We must make immediate arrangements to ship out. First and foremost, all the treasure must be moved from the strongholds and be buried in these three locations." He handed each one a map and gave orders to assign a detail to each location. No one from each of the three parties was to share information with the other, and all maps were to be returned to Gilcox.

"We must make the natives believe we are taking the treasure with us and that we'll not be returning. The fact is that we will not return for some time, but when we do return, it will be at the opportune time to pick up the treasure. For now, we will sail north to plunder English colonies and ships carrying taxes back to England."

Stroppy Newsome spoke up for the others. "And what then, Cap'n? Ah we destined to nevah lay a bed roll on terra firma again?" Giddy glared at Newsome, and his bosun apologetically asked, "Beggin' ya pardon, sah, we just wants ta know what might 'appen next."

Giddy glanced at the other two to gauge their reaction. They kept their eyes down, leaving Newsome to hang on his own. Gilcox had too much on his mind to deal further with Newsome and responded coolly, "Suffice it to say, Mr. Newsome, there is always a plan, and when any buccaneer needs to know, I will educate him. Now, you have your orders."

~~~

Northwest of Albatross in Jamaica, Lieutenant Commander Leslie Christian sat at his desk, rereading the letter from the governor. This was just the information he needed to complete the preparation for capturing the pirate Gilcox. He knew that sooner or later, clues would surface about the pirate's whereabouts.

With the letter in hand, he jumped up and went directly to the window. Anger began to boil up from within him as he observed his crew's poor effort at stocking the ship.

"Bloody damn hell," the lieutenant hissed. It looked as though another storm was brewing on the horizon. He slammed his hand against the window jam and gritted his teeth in anger at the ineptitude of his crew. *What the hell is wrong with them? We should have been under sail four days ago.*

He called his first mate into the room. "Mr. Wilson, what in the world is happening? Why all the delays? Why are we not out to sea as yet?"

Wilson was sweating and drew a breath in frustration. He removed his hat and said in an apologetic tone, "Well, sir, many of the men have fallen ill from spoiled rations. We are now at work replacing the rations."

Christian shot back, "I don't believe it! How many odd events could possibly happen to one ship? I want you to get to the bottom of this, or I have a mind to scourge every last one of this miserable crew."

Wilson hesitated a moment before speaking again. "Lieutenant, sir, I'm afraid the truth may have more to do with fear."

"What is it, man?" Christian demanded. "What is it you're trying to say?"

"Sir," began the first mate reluctantly, "many of the men—the officers right down to the cabin boy—have admitted that they have no desire to approach Albatross, let alone take on the devil Giddy Gilcox."

"Are you telling me that this crew has deliberately acted derelict in their duties to avoid going after this pirate?"

"Yes, sir," Wilson admitted, "it is my opinion that what you say is true."

Christian seethed but controlled his anger. "Gather the men together. I shall make my case on the importance of this mission. Then I shall threaten to put them all in irons for blatant dereliction of duty if we are not underway by the first week of October. To make my point clear, we shall administer twenty lashes to several of the crew who feigned sickness. We shall see how they like their medicine. I assure you that if that scoundrel Gilcox escapes, this entire crew will face even worse medicine."

With the lieutenant's motivation, by early October, the man-of-war HMS *Sovereign*, primed for engagement, set sail on a southeasterly course for Albatross Island.

Chapter Eight

Giddy was angry. He tried to study his maps but could not. Pacing around his hut like a caged animal, he stewed over his frustrations with his crew. At one point, he looked up and caught sight of his reflection in a looking glass that hung on the wall. The stab of pain he felt caused him to pull his dagger and throw it at the mirror. The glass exploded, leaving the dagger planted quivering in the wall.

Newsome was intolerable, and at times, Gilcox wanted to keel-haul every one of the crew for their stupidity. Now he was faced with having to abandon his glorious island home. He had known it was inevitable that they would have to leave one day, but where would they end up? He was the lord of this island, and the only other home he had ever known before was filled with pain and anguish.

The *Rogue Flattery* was his true love. She was absolutely the fastest, most nimble craft to sail the open sea. He was her creator and lord, and she was his mistress. Yet even she would have to be replaced one day.

Giddy could remember a time when he felt safe. Even as a boy, after he was disfigured, there had been a safe place where he could hide away. The feeling he'd had over the years on this island reminded him of that childhood sanctuary. Eventually, his childhood lair had been discovered, and it changed his life forever.

As a youngster, Giddy spent a great deal of time at his father's business, Gilcox & Woodrow, Shipbuilders Ltd., as his mother refused to be faced with the disappointment of her son during the daylight hours, even with the bag that served as a mask over his head. After a while, even that was fine with Giddy. Behind the closed doors of his father's office, he dreamt of the sea as he looked from the window at the shipbuilding activity and the docks of Portsmouth. He would stay cloistered in his father's office, poring over the designers' work, whiling away the hours reading about sailing or designing and then building his own ship models. When he would venture out during the evening, certain no one was around, he would sail his models by moonlight in a nearby pond.

Young Giddy's solitude was shattered one day when the son of his father's partner, Ian Woodrow, discovered him. Ian was several years older than Giddy. He was forced by an overbearing father to come to the Gilcox & Woodrow offices to perform menial tasks. Ian did not want to be there to begin with, and he certainly didn't want to perform these boring activities that he felt were beneath him. When he discovered Giddy, he found an object on which to release his frustration and with which to entertain himself.

Immediately, the young Woodrow began to abuse Giddy. He would sneak into the office, steal Giddy's mask, and then belittle Giddy, calling him names such as Ghastly Giddy and Ugly Ox Gilcox. The older boy felt as though he had the right to treat Giddy like an unwanted dog, slapping, punching, and kicking him.

Giddy was heckled and abused by many, but there was no more evil and severe treatment toward young Gilcox than that of Ian Woodrow. Yet even with the extent of Ian's treatment, Giddy's most painful experiences came when he would turn to his own father to intervene and comfort him. His father's only response would be, "Horacio Gilcox, a life of this treatment lies ahead of you. You must learn to live with it."

As he grew older, Gilcox yearned to escape from this world to a life on the open sea. He begged his father to use his influence to arrange for a position on one of the Gilcox-built ships. His father agreed—he saw this as a relief from the guilt and anxiety he and his wife felt due to Giddy's presence.

At age seventeen, Giddy was given a small cabin with light duty, maintaining the officers' quarters on an eight-hundred-ton East Indiamen merchant ship bound for India. As the strange shipmate hidden under a cloth mask, Giddy initially spooked the crew, but during the late-night watch, he would offer to take over some of the most undesirable duties from the crew, which they would gladly relinquish. His hard work and knowledge of both ship and sea impressed the crew.

One shipmate, in particular, went out of his way to include Giddy when the crew was off duty. Christopher Thomas would not allow the others to chide Giddy or to "take the mickey out of 'im." One day, Thomas even visited Giddy in his cabin, taking great interest in Giddy and his things. Giddy was beside himself, for he had never had this kind of contact before. *Is this friendship?* he wondered.

But then, at the very next port of call along the Ivory Coast, Christopher Thomas disappeared—along with everything of any value that Giddy had brought with him.

It was just another one of life's painful lessons, teaching Giddy that love, caring, and friendship were not true sentiments. Perhaps devotion to duty was a genuine sentiment, but the others were only feelings that were easily faked to manipulate fools as a way to achieve selfish desires. He would never take kind words or gestures seriously again. The power of flattery from a rogue, however, was a weapon he would learn to brandish with great skill.

Still, on this voyage, Giddy had established contacts with capable sailors. Many were obviously common folk, not very bright but often dangerous. Violence was not a foreign idea to them. Often, they were out at sea to escape trouble at home. They had seen it all, and Giddy's appearance did not seem to trouble sailors as much as it did landlubbers.

First Mate Darby Blackbury, if indeed that was his name, was one such sailor. He had served on merchant ships for eighteen years. He was big, strong, hard-working, quick-tempered, and devoted to his duty—yet he was a man who cared so deeply about his family that he decided to give up the long months away at sea to find a career on land. He had joined the king's army based on the promise that he would remain stationed among the British Isles. Instead, he was immediately shipped overseas.

After consecutive campaigns in Europe and Africa, he'd had enough of the broken promises—and he snapped, killing his enlisting officer. He found passage back to England, but when he arrived, he found his family gone, decimated by a great disease that had swept through the slums that summer. Lonely and delirious from his grief, he was apprehended for stealing food from a wealthy family. Darby then escaped by killing two guards before he could be identified for his previous crimes.

Blackbury knew then exactly where he could go to disappear— back to the merchant traders who were always desperate for able-bodied men and who never asked questions. He signed on to the same first voyage that Giddy Gilcox had served on. Giddy, as well as the officers on board, could see that Blackbury was capable and devoted to duty, and his strength in meeting any physical challenge was impressive. Blackbury kept to himself and never seemed to notice or care about Giddy's strange appearance.

Darby moved up the ranks as a seaman and enjoyed higher pay and greater privileges. After the first voyage, Giddy arranged for Blackbury to sign on to one voyage after another so that he barely stepped foot on British soil and so avoided being apprehended for his crimes. Giddy would make good use of this man one day.

Chapter Nine

Young Giddy Gilcox shipped out on numerous voyages and quickly learned the ins and outs of each ship better than any man on board. The crew knew—as did Giddy himself—that he could captain better than any of the men he served under. He also continued to establish contacts with his shipmates on each voyage, keeping a log of names, seamanship skills, and other talents for future reference.

On Giddy's last voyage on the open sea, while returning from China, the ship's officers all took deathly ill from poisoning. Whether or not it was coincidental, no one knew. The crew turned to Giddy for leadership, and as they sailed home, all noted a vast improvement in the ship's handling. The ship returned to England's shores a full week earlier than scheduled.

That was it for Giddy—he had to captain his own ship. But even through his father's contacts, he could not overcome the ship owners' abhorrence of his physical appearance. Giddy became even angrier and more reclusive. With his years at sea and constant study and modeling of new ship designs, Giddy threw himself into designing and building the fastest and ablest ship ever to sail.

His final design was far more advanced than any ship ever built. Though she was somewhat smaller than other ships he had worked on, there would be no ship as sleek and swift as his. The designs of the day provided for wide ships with square bows that plowed over the waves. But his design was a slender craft, several times longer than she was wide. The bow was sharper, and the stern was slim and tapered so she could slip through the water with little fuss. In addition, her masts were taller, with much bigger yards and sails.

Giddy convinced his father of his ship's prowess. Gilcox & Woodrow was struggling, and because his father hoped that this new design might restore the firm's waning prominence, he agreed to build it. All the other shipbuilders and seadogs scoffed at the design—they were certain that the ship would sink when hit with her first heavy sea. Some within Gilcox & Woodrow also disagreed with Giddy's design.

Mr. Woodrow had passed away a year earlier, and young Ian Woodrow had taken his father's position in the firm. Over the years, Ian's mean spirit and evil temperament had disappeared. Now, he was kinder and even made attempts to make amends with Giddy.

But Giddy would have none of it. The tables had turned, and Giddy, with his superior intellect, took every opportunity to embarrass Ian. The young Woodrow made no attempt to retaliate and accepted the treatment as his due. When it came to this new design, though, Ian felt compelled to speak up. He claimed to be genuinely concerned for the safety of those who would sail the ship. The design was too radical a departure, and he feared disaster.

As the project moved ahead, Giddy's father made it known that he would choose another captain—not Giddy—to sail the ship on her test voyage. This was the last straw for Giddy. In public, he took the news stoically, but in his heart, he was determined to steal the ship away and start a completely new chapter in his life.

His plan was to work diligently and heartily to complete the ship. Before the captain was chosen, he volunteered to personally oversee the selection of the crew. His handpicked crew was made up of the best he had sailed with and those he knew would follow him eagerly as a sailor of fortune. Giddy even convinced his father to allow him to load the ship, as if preparing for a long voyage, to fully test her capabilities in the open sea.

As he became more exposed to the public, their rejection and repulsion of Giddy fueled his anger and determination even further. He swallowed the pain deep, where it sat and festered. He responded to those around him with polite acquiescence and flattery, but inwardly, he laughed at them, for he knew that they would all have real reason to fear him one day.

Any opposition to the ship's design or to its completion was met with the same polite demeanor. But anyone who stood in Giddy's way ultimately met with illness, accident, or even death—so much so that rumor circulated concerning a curse that had been put upon the project. The first to fall victim to the curse was Ian Woodrow. While in the shipyard one day, searching the ship's development for flaws, a huge block mysteriously dropped from its tackle and crushed him to death.

Even with the great public interest in the new design, only the Gilcoxes and the crew were allowed on the test voyage. When the day finally arrived, and just before the newly named *Righteous Gale* was due to set sail, Mr. Gilcox received a note from his son that he had taken ill. In the note, Giddy insisted that the test voyage still should go on without him. His father did not hesitate, for even he was beginning to suspect that his son might be the one who had brought the curse upon the project. He commissioned the captain to proceed, and the *Righteous Gale* was warped from the harbor and quickly opened up to full sail.

Almost immediately, she was clipping along at such a pace that the knot rope proved too short to measure her speed. She was a handful for the crew to sail, like a wild stallion galloping freely beneath them. At about eight leagues out to sea, Bosun Stroppy Newsome reported that some rigging had broken free, threatening to tear sails and break the foremast yards.

The captain gave the order to "heave to," and the ship was slowed to a stop. The mates gathered to begin repairs—and then, without warning, the crew turned and murdered the unsuspecting officers, throwing their bodies overboard. Mr. Gilcox was captured, taken below, and bound to a chair.

Shortly thereafter, a small sloop with three men on board arrived alongside the ship. The new officers boarded the ship and claimed her as a pirate vessel, renamed the *Rogue Flattery*. She would now be captained by one Giddy Gilcox.

The new captain gave orders to sink the sloop and set sail west to the Americas. Immediately, the crew jumped to their stations and began chanting the sailor songs that crews had chanted for centuries. This was a new start for them all. Each one was leaving behind a troubled past, and they all were united in seeking a new beginning.

Giddy tore off his mask and turned his face to the wind. This mask had become such a part of him that he sometimes would forget to take it off, even during his private hours. Yet it represented all that was unfair to him in life, and he vowed to never wear it again. More than that, he swore that anyone who ever again made him feel that he should cover his face would pay a horrible price for it.

Giddy now had the ship of his dreams, a crew capable and determined to find adventure and fortune, and a full store of provisions to get them across the Atlantic. All else he left behind, including his bondage that had been embodied by a cloth sack, which now floated over the sea off England's western shores.

This was the same bondage he'd left in a small bedroom at the back of his father's house in Portsmouth, the bondage created by a society that couldn't see beyond his outward appearance.

Now, with the cool, damp evening breeze coursing over his exposed face, Giddy thought he felt freedom for the first time. Yet there was something gnawing at him that told him that this wasn't real freedom, and it wouldn't last. Still, it felt so good, as good as he had ever known. He was determined to hang on to it for as long as his cracked and wart-covered hands could hold.

There was one other thing that Giddy left behind: a note prominently displayed on his drafting table was discovered several days after the *Righteous Gale* was to have returned. It read as follows:

> My worst fears have been realized! *Righteous Gale* has not returned, and the guilt overwhelms me. My desire to build the swiftest craft to ever sail blinded me to a flawed design. In my heart, I knew this craft would buckle under large waves. So certain was I of this fact that I could not bring myself to step aboard her to make the fateful voyage and so feigned illness. The lives of the entire crew, as well as of my own father, weigh heavy upon my conscience. My guilt will surely overcome my cowardice to put my own self away. Until then, I depart to never return.
>
> God rest these souls in a place I know I will never see the light of.
>
> Horacio Gilcox

Giddy knew that his note would accomplish several things. First, it would further convince the seafaring community that Giddy's design was faulty and erase any doubt as to how the ship was lost. Second, it would explain to the authorities that Giddy was at fault and that justice would take care of itself. And third, it would guarantee that this "faulty" ship design would not be replicated for a long time to come.

Captain Gilcox had made a clean escape, and his plan left no cause for criminal investigation, no need for a search party, and no outstanding bounty upon his head. The seafaring community already had decided that Giddy was cursed and that his design was a failure. This "tragedy" convinced them of how right they were. Only Giddy and his crew knew that he had outsmarted them all.

Chapter Ten

On Albatross, the captain busied himself by overseeing all the preparations for their departure from the island. The treasure chests, filled with rocks and dirt, were ceremoniously paraded toward the ship, in full view of the natives, so that they would believe the treasure was actually leaving the island. Already, much of the salvaged rum—the portion the captain allowed the crew to keep—had been stored on the ship. Giddy's library, as well as all of the necessary provisions and ammunition, had already been stowed away.

"Mr. Blackbury!" Gilcox called out from the quarterdeck down to the dock. "Remove those native wives. They are slowing our progress, and I detest their emotional outbursts."

Stroppy Newsome, standing near the captain, commented under his breath, "Aye, Cap'n, but it does mean that our permanent departure is most convincing."

"Very astute of you, Mr. Newsome," Giddy conceded. Looking back down at Blackbury, he ordered, "Now, call the men together in the waist. I want to address them before our departure."

The crew formed just below where Giddy stood on the quarterdeck. Their captain peered down menacingly at them through his deep, sunken eyes. He waited for them to quiet under his stare before he spoke. "Well, my miserable soldiers of fortune, the time has come for us to move from our buccaneer haven. Many of you have been murmuring, and it's time I told you why we must leave behind so perfect a sea fortress. We have been discovered.

"The ship log of the *Cane's Burden*, found several weeks ago, shows that their captain spied us entering the island and reported it to the authorities. I am certain that the navy is bearing down on us at this very moment."

The men grew uneasy. One of them had failed to do his duty, and Gilcox and his officers already knew who it was. "Squirrel" Birmingham had been in the crow's nest at the time they had entered the channel to the lagoon. He was nicknamed "Squirrel" for his ability to scamper up rigging and live amongst the highest yards. Most of the crew preferred to spend time on deck and were happy to allow him to do the high work, and Squirrel would take this duty as often as possible to avoid what he considered the harder duty on deck.

Gilcox had suspected that he was not much of a lookout, for it appeared that he could adeptly sleep on his feet, and he rarely reported much. The captain also noticed that the last time the *Rogue Flattery* had been pulled into the channel, Squirrel was the first one off the ship.

This slacker's days with the crew were surely numbered. As the captain outlined his plan, he noticed Squirrel slip off behind the galley to the forecastle and then climb over the rail and down a line to the water. Giddy would allow him to hide under the dock until the ship and Squirrel's pirate mates were gone.

Gilcox planned for Squirrel to flee, and he was prepared to leave the sailor on the island. In fact, he fully expected Squirrel's capture by Lieutenant Christian and hoped the pirate would freely divulge their plan to the English captain. Gilcox would then be in complete command of his destiny. As Christian pursued the pirates, Giddy Gilcox would find the right moment to convert his pursuer's zeal to his own advantage.

At high tide, the *Rogue Flattery* was warped away from the dock.

The anchor was rowed out by longboat and dropped into the channel, followed by the crew's hauling in the anchor rope, inching the ship along the channel. This was repeated several times until the ship was out in the open sea.

Like the wild sea stallion that she was, the *Rogue Flattery* immediately leapt into a full gallop as the crew fed her frenzy with more and more snapping white sail. Kicking up the blue, frothy sod, she boldly proclaimed, "Catch me if you can!" To Gilcox, she was an exhilarating vision of the unbound freedom that drew him and other adventurous men to the dangers of the wild sea.

~~~

Lieutenant Commander Leslie Christian sat in his quarters surveying charts, looking for something that wasn't there. He suddenly threw his compass down in frustration. As he stood looking at his broken compass, he heard a knock on his door. "Enter," he grumbled.

First Mate Wilson entered the room and cheerfully reported, "Good news, Captain. We've spotted Albatross Island."

Christian felt some relief, but he was still not pleased. "In record time, I might add. This voyage, Mr. Wilson, has been an exercise in pure frustration."

Wilson felt the need to explain and responded, "I'm afraid, Captain, it has been a string of bad fortune. Unfavorable winds, ongoing need for repairs, fighting amongst the marines, and a distressed crew and vessel, which we could not avoid repairing, added days to our sailing time."

"Yes, Mr. Wilson, I know all that. The excuses do not ease my displeasure." Having put voice to his frustrations, Christian's mood began to improve. "Now, at least we do have Albatross in our sight." He pointed to the chart. "You will bring the ship to the northwest of the island, keeping a good distance to avoid her reefs. Drop the longboats and deploy a sailor for each boat with the marines. I shall lead the shore party, and you shall take command of the ship. We shall row east around the island and closer to the location where the pirate ship was reported to have disappeared."

"Sir," Wilson added, "because of the dangerous rocks and coral reefs, we'll be too far out to anchor."

"Yes," Christian agreed. "To avoid detection, if we haven't been spotted already, you will be required to sail out farther and circle back regularly for our return."

Later, with the two boats loaded, Christian handed the ship over to his second in command, saying, "Mr. Wilson, you are now in command of the ship. Keep a sharp eye out for any strange ships coming from within or around the island. My orders for you are to not engage the pirates unless absolutely necessary."

Chapter Eleven

Commander Leslie Christian, twenty-one marines, and two sailors set off in two boats, rowing the mile-long distance to shore, expecting to be met either by pirates or natives when they landed. They searched but could not find one place any better than another to land. The boats had difficulty managing the heavy surf, and both turned over into the water near shore. Fortunately, there was no enemy to greet them. Every member of the landing crew was soaked, along with all their weapons and powder. It took the full remainder of the day to pull everything out of the water, dry it all, and ready themselves for the assault. Many of their firearms were never recovered.

Later that night, with the moon at its highest, Christian ordered, "Sergeant Fulton, if your men are ready, let's move out."

"Aye, Captain," Fulton replied, "my marines are ready."

Christian turned to the sailors. "You men stay here to guard the boats. Be ready to shove off on a moment's notice."

The lieutenant commander and the marine sergeant silently led the party southeastward along the beach until they came to the channel that led to the lagoon.

Christian was amazed that a channel of this size had never been spotted from the sea. The shore party moved inland along the edge of the channel, and just before sunrise, they arrived at the lagoon.

As they came to the end of the channel, Christian was further surprised to see what a fine port it was and how fully equipped and organized it appeared. He stopped to survey the situation and huddled up the marines to outline assignments for the attack.

"Cap'n, sah," Fulton spoke up, "where da ya s'pose da pirate ship is at?"

Before Christian could outline his plan of attack, he looked into the marine's face, then jumped up to survey the lagoon. Christian's face flushed. He had been so caught up in finding the secret cove he failed to recognize that there was no ship there. "All right, men," Christian spoke up, "it appears that the ship—and in all likelihood, the pirates—are out to sea. Let's move quickly, but cautiously, into their camp and see what we can find out concerning their whereabouts. Step lively now!"

The shore party moved into the camp, and Christian continued to be shocked by the sophistication of this port "village". It looked as though it had just been ransacked, with things scattered all about. There was no resistance or any sign of life, but as they peered into each hut and cabin, they found natives asleep and obviously under the influence, with rum kegs all about.

The shore party then came upon what looked to be the captain's quarters. A fence surrounded it, made up of fine pieces of carved wood, but as Christian started to pass through it, he stopped suddenly and stepped quickly back. His heart stopped, and a nauseous feeling arose in his stomach.

He ran his fingers over some of the wood pieces as tears filled his eyes. There before him was a fence made up entirely of ship name-plates. He scanned the names and began to recognize ships that he knew had disappeared without a trace—ships that had carried relatives, friends, shipmates, and classmates. He now had before him the sad answer to the mysterious disappearances had offered some hope that these people were still alive.

Up to this point in time, Giddy Gilcox had represented Christian's chance for adventure, fame, prestige, and possibly fortune. Now, this great opportunity was turned into personal rage and hatred. The captain charged through the gate and into Giddy's cabin, with his sword raised in one hand and a pistol drawn in the other. He charged in alone, as if intending to take on the whole heathen horde of pirates himself.

Bursting through the door, Christian found Squirrel, still liquored and fast asleep, with his native wife. The woman immediately started screaming, then jumped up and grabbed a rum keg. She lifted it over her head to throw at Christian. He deflected the barrel with his sword and shot the screaming woman through the neck. She fell to the floor, gasping for air. Squirrel only shifted his body in bed and remained asleep, murmuring, "'Twern't me, Cap'n. Squirrel 'as an eagle eye. I done my duty, I done."

Sergeant Fulton calmly stepped into the cabin, quickly surveyed the situation, and in his heavy cockney accent, said, "Well done, Cap'n. I fink you got dese pirates onna run!"

Christian glared at him and ordered, "Drag this stinking scoundrel pirate outside and do what you must to sober him up."

By the time Christian came out of the cabin, Squirrel was soaked with water and sitting in a mud puddle. As he began to speak, Christian walked over and immediately gave him a swift kick to his stomach. Squirrel sputtered and choked.

Christian continued kicking Squirrel and beating him with the butt of his pistol. When he was exhausted, he ordered more buckets of water to be thrown on the prisoner, and then had him dragged and propped up against a tree.

Christian squatted down next to the pirate. "Now, my fine fellow, that will be just the beginning if you do not tell me where your pirate brethren are!"

Squirrel simply shrugged his shoulders and shook his head. When he looked up at Christian, the commander flinched. It was a look Christian had never seen. There was a haunting fear in the man's eyes—fear that went much deeper than the physical pain being inflicted upon him.

The navy commander pulled Fulton aside and whispered, "Mr. Fulton, do you see what I see in that man's eyes?"

Fulton was quick to respond. "There's a sickness there, Cap'n. I never seen nuffin' like 'at afore. He ain't afraid of us, I tell ya that. I've heard that da devil Gilcox holds extraordinary power over his men—mystical powers."

"Indeed," Christian agreed. "I believe Gilcox's very presence is haunting this man's every breath. There's a reason why this man was left behind, and I have a feeling he's been cursed for it. Let us see if we can get his attention."

Christian turned and knelt in front of Squirrel. He lowered his head, outstretched his hand with an open palm, and said to no one in particular, "A gully knife, please."

A soldier handed him a folded knife. While Christian opened the knife, he said, "I do not believe you heard me correctly, so perhaps I can assist you."

Grabbing Squirrel's right ear between his thumb and index finger, he took a swipe with the knife and cut his ear clean off.

Squirrel flinched and reacted with a wince and a grunt, as if to say, *Bloody hell! Why did ya 'ave ta do 'at fo'?*

Christian held the ear up before the pirate and calmly said, "Now, there are many more parts that will be much more painful to live without. 'Fess up."

Christian had always found a severed ear to be one of the most effective tools to replace any other thought a prisoner might be dwelling upon. Seeing his ear in front of him made Squirrel crack, and he divulged all he knew about the pirates' plans to sail north and plunder the coastal colonies. When Christian heard that Giddy was after British taxes, he knew where they were headed, and he started to formulate his own plan.

While their attention was drawn to Christian, Squirrel slowly stood up, turned, and scampered right up the tree. The marines all turned and started to shout. Several sent their swords slicing at the tree just below Squirrel's feet.

Stepping back, the sergeant spoke in amazement, "Blimey, the bugger can climb fasta than I kin run!"

Christian was not pleased, but the marines began to laugh at what seemed to be a foolish attempt to escape, as there was nowhere for the pirate to go. The lieutenant's irritation grew as they watched Squirrel scamper across one limb and onto another of an adjacent tree. It soon became apparent that the pirate could cover quite a bit of ground and possibly get to the lagoon, where they might never catch him.

Christian had had enough and ordered one of the marines to shoot and bring him down. One by one, the marines shot and missed, as Squirrel adroitly ducked behind branches and limbs. Their frustration grew, as Squirrel started to mock them with wild laughter, bird calls, and animal sounds. They chased him until the trees thinned out.

Christian's frustration began to boil over as he ordered, "Sergeant, organize your men into a ring of fire and bring that cursed animal down."

Fulton set his men in a circle around the tree and ordered, "Fire!"

Squirrel's body did a little jig before he came tumbling down, bouncing off branches and landing on his neck, dead. The men joked and laughed as they stood over his twisted body.

Chapter Twelve

"Quiet!" Christian ordered.

The whole shore party began to notice movement in the brush around them. All the commotion about Squirrel had drawn the island natives to the camp, and the forest was now seemingly alive.

"Retreat back to the boats, men," Christian said calmly.

Slowly and deliberately, the men collected their belongings and headed toward the channel. Leslie Christian could feel his heart begin to pound. Even though he had dismissed the stories, the rumors of the dangers on the island were still firmly embedded in his mind.

Up to this point, he had felt confident. There had been no real resistance and no sign of the black magic for which the island was well known. But a darkness and fear gripped him.

They moved quickly back the way they had come along the channel. The captain halted the platoon to confer with the sergeant. The men bunched up together, eyes darting all about, fear and anxiety reflected in every face. The captain and the sergeant agreed that to go to the beach and follow it back to the boats would likely take longer and leave them exposed on the open beach. They decided they would move directly north through the forest.

They started out, moving at an even pace, with Christian leading the way. He began to sense the growing presence of the natives all around them, and his pace quickened. Suddenly, a flurry of objects began to rain down on them. He could hear small arrows zing through the air, followed by crisp smacks against the trees. One of the men jerked to the side, grabbed his neck, stumbled a few steps, and collapsed.

Christian did not hesitate and broke into a run. The whole party didn't need instruction. They followed in a panicked frenzy, dropping water, powder, and even some muskets to lighten their load. If any had looked back, they would have seen that one by one, the line of marines was getting shorter. Some of the men were indiscriminately firing their muskets and pistols behind them as they ran, likely dwindling their numbers even further.

Christian felt his legs weakening. He gasped for air in the heat, sweating and dehydrated. Only his adrenaline kept him from fainting dead away.

The sergeant, right behind Christian, choked out, "Cap'n, shud we make a stand?"

Christian answered only with "Forward!" as he waved his hand to the north.

The only hope he held for any of them was to get to the boats. Christian began to slow from exhaustion. He turned to look behind him and saw that their numbers seemed to have stabilized. The presence of the natives was no longer as strong as it had been. Still, Christian pushed them on, fueled by the gripping fear of the unknown evil, until finally he broke through the thick jungle to the beach.

Christian found himself on top of a fifteen-foot bluff with a narrow strip of beach below. He quickly waved at each man to jump down. Without more than a quick hesitation to gauge where to land, they each jumped and tumbled down to the beach, with Christian bringing up the rear. Once on the beach, they all scrambled to the water's edge and hid behind large boulders for cover.

After they had a minute to collect themselves, it dawned on Christian that he was not sure if they had emerged before or beyond where the boats lay.

He heard the sergeant ask, "Which way, Cap'n?"

Without a moment of hesitation, and with a tone of complete confidence, the captain pointed northwest. "This way, men. Our rescue awaits!"

As they trotted along the water's edge, Christian wracked his brain to see if he recognized any of the terrain or if he could catch a glimpse of the boats or maybe even the ship. He was uncertain which way to turn, but he figured that he was more likely to run into the natives if they circled back south. To his great relief, as they turned a sharp bend, they saw the boats. They were still some distance away, but he could see one of the sailors, left to guard the boats, hammering at the boat in mid-repair.

Christian's first reaction was anger. Didn't this fool know that such a great noise could bring the savages down upon them? He wanted to yell to the man but knew it would be fruitless. As the men came closer, Christian noticed something strange—the sailor didn't appear to be wearing leggings. Just then, a native stood up from behind the boat, intently looking over the hull. These were not the sailors, Christian realized, but natives, sabotaging their escape.

The captain turned to the sergeant. "Can you get a clean shot off from here?"

Fulton nodded his head and grabbed a loaded musket. Dropping to one knee while licking his thumb and cleaning the sight, he took aim. Drawing a breath, he squeezed the trigger. *BANG!* The ball hit a bone in the native's wrist, blowing off part of his hand and sending his upraised hatchet flying.

The entire group froze for a moment in amazement. Christian, too, was stunned by the sergeant's accuracy. "Bloody good show!" he said in disbelief, and then followed his remark with a long scream of

"Chaaaaarge!"

The depleted party cheered and raced to the boats. Christian was encouraged as he saw the natives dive into the woods, but his exhilaration was dashed when they arrived at the boats. The sailors lay bludgeoned and stripped of their belongings. One boat was completely destroyed, but the savages had obviously just started their work on the other, leaving a hole about the size of a small scupper.

This scene, coupled with the fact that HMS *Sovereign* was nowhere in sight, caused Christian's heart to sink. For all he knew, the pirates had attacked and sunk their ship. He looked over at the men as they stared out to sea and saw the same expression of anxious fear on all of their faces.

~~~

Christian had the men gather together, and they huddled between the two boats. He was determined they would survive this ordeal and wanted to come up with words to encourage the disheartened marines. The commander looked at the dead sailors, and the thought occurred to him that if they had arrived just minutes earlier, these men would still be alive, and their own chances would have been much improved. He cursed to himself, realizing that this excursion had been a disaster— poorly planned, impetuously conceived, and operating under the notion that if they just showed up, the pirates would surrender.

At that moment, Lieutenant Commander Leslie Christian resolved to redeem himself and survive. He would save as many of the remaining men as possible, regain his command, and finish the task of putting an end to Giddy Gilcox and his cutthroats.

He spoke up with an air of control and confidence to lift the men's spirits. "Men, the *Sovereign* shall return soon. We can repair this boat and be out to meet her in no time. Our contingent's numbers have been trimmed enough that only one boat will be required. Sergeant, collect all gully knives, bayonets, water pouches, and any loose clothing you can find. We can use what we have to repair the remaining boat."

Christian's words seemed to raise the men's hopes, and they quickly went to work gathering the items for the boat's repair.

Cutting a water pouch fully open, Christian spread it over the hole from the outside. Then, breaking the knife and bayonet tips off, he used them to nail some of the larger, loose boards over the hole. From the inside, he stuffed the loose garments into the hole to make the repairs as tight as possible. The boat would require constant bailing, but it was ready.

With the repairs completed, Christian ordered the men into the boat. The men anxiously pushed her into the surf, struggling to get through the heavy waves. Just when they were beyond the surf, one of the men pointed southward, shouting, "Look!"

Christian turned to their starboard and spotted a host of native canoes racing toward them. He immediately shouted, "Pull with all your might, men!"

He hoped that they could outrun them, but the canoes were moving swiftly, and he gauged that it wouldn't be long before they would be overtaken.

To add to their problems, the repair was leaking badly and required constant attention, which further slowed them down. Christian was just about to order them to come about and take their chances back in the forest when they heard a loud concussion, followed by a geyser of water some twenty yards from the natives.

Christian turned to his left and saw the *Sovereign* coming into view around the point, guns blazing. The men all cheered while their commander repeated, "Pull with all your might, men. We can outrun these savages!"

The natives, however, showed no sign of slowing their pace. Another volley fell even closer to the savages, but it was also closer to their own boat. Christian became anxious when it dawned on him that most of the gunners on board the ship were untested in battle. He could not vouch for their accuracy, and his gunners were firing over their heads at the natives closing in on them.

He looked up just as the next volley passed right over the marines' heads before slamming into the water just past their boat. The resulting swell rolled the boat over on its larboard side, and all those in the boat lost their balance. The boat was swamped and swiftly disappeared under the waves.

The next shot hit squarely among the native canoes, and they immediately retreated back to the island. Christian and the remaining marines struggled to swim toward the ship; they were met by another boat from *Sovereign*, sent to fish them from the sea.

As the commander climbed aboard his ship, the crew stood at attention. Christian noticed a look of surprise upon many of his sailors' faces. It was then he realized that even more men had been lost when their boat sank. He took a quick count—of a shore party of twenty-one, only nine had returned.

Christian was stunned by the realization of how significant was the loss of his men. He stiffened and straightened his wet uniform. He would not show his discouragement to the crew and returned the salute of his first mate. The command of the ship was now restored to him.

The remnants of the marines huddled by the forecastle while the ship's doctor brought food and patched their wounds.

Later that evening, back in his element, Christian strolled the deck as they sailed back to Jamaica. He sought out Sergeant Fulton to commend him for his good service. The sergeant sat with his knees to his chest and with his back up against the bulkhead on the main deck.

Though it appeared that the sergeant had no intention of rising to salute, the captain said, "Sergeant, please stay at ease. You and your men are to be commended for facing such a dangerous mission with stiff-necked bravery. I plan to report directly to the royal governor when we put in to Jamaica and recommend citations for you all. Job well done!"

He waited for a response, but the sergeant only looked up, and Christian could see his red, swollen eyes in the bright moonlight—

eyes that told the story of a decimated company of men who had accomplished nothing but killing one drunken pirate, shooting a native woman, and wounding one hostile native in the hand. Christian knew what the sergeant's eyes were saying and chose not to wait to hear it verbalized; he quickly excused himself.

Christian only wanted to think that he had been successful in exacting valuable information about the pirates' plans. He would sail ahead of Gilcox to where he was certain the pirate was headed. Though he knew that he would have to be more diligent in thinking through every detail, with the information he had gathered, he now felt he had an advantage over the pirate.

Lieutenant Commander Leslie Christian swore under his breath, "By God, I will put an end to this dirty scoundrel."

Christian looked up at the moon. He now felt an assurance that his plans to capture the pirate were as certain as the Caribbean sea breeze passing over the full, white moon.

This is my destiny, he thought. *Surely this is the destiny of the* Sovereign, *her captain, and his crew.*

Chapter Thirteen

Helen Tanner sat on a stone bench, humming and rocking back and forth while sewing a great piece of cloth draped over her lap and down her legs. She watched her young son, five years of age, frolicking in the backyard pond, as active and as happy as a spawning fish. She stopped her sewing and looked around her. The idyllic life the Tanners had established in the Virginia colony made her chest swell with pride and joy. She didn't want this picture to ever change.

How more blessed could any woman be? she thought. *Truly blessed; I've a loving husband who is proud father to our bright and healthy son. We have position and influence in the Williamsburg community and a wonderful home with caring servants who are like family.*

Helen's ears perked up at the sound of someone's whistling a familiar tune from behind her. Without hesitation, she lifted her face and, with closed eyes, whistled back a refrain. She turned and beamed a smile at her husband, William.

William stood leaning against a tree. He grabbed his chest, sighed deeply, and then said, "God bless ye, Helen of joy, mother of my sweet little boy."

Her response was, as always, "William, I do tell, for your lass and our boy, all is well!"

It was a greeting they repeatedly used with each other and one that never ceased to warm her heart.

William called out, "Come, my love, come into the house. Young William, you come, too. I have some wonderful, exciting news to share."

Helen quickly dried off her son and met her husband at the tree. They turned to walk back into the house, with young William trailing behind.

William put his arms around his wife and said, "I stood spying on you for several minutes, you know."

"Oh, really? And what did you learn?"

"Nothing very new, simply confirmation that my God has provided me with a helpmate perfectly crafted by His very hands."

She blushed, feeling embarrassed to respond.

"You are a precious jewel without any imperfection," he continued, "all good, gentle, and kind. I truly do not believe you are capable of an evil thought or deed, so much so that you make me strive to be a better man and a better Christian. If ever I saw the goodness of God embodied in human flesh, it is in you, my dear wife. You are selfless, caring, loving, and always cheerful. I am made to realize how undeserving I am of not only God's love but also of yours."

The words were too much for her, and she answered, "William, you will make me faint away with such flattery—so much flattery that I am tempted to become suspicious of the news you are preparing me for."

William smiled. "Oh, it is all so true, yet you highlight the fact that I failed to acknowledge your brilliant mind as well."

Helen returned his smile. "William, you are the most beautiful scoundrel."

As they entered the house, Helen took a seat and put young William on her lap. The boy immediately began to play with the gold charm hanging from the necklace draped around her neck. William began to pace back and forth as he spoke, seeming like a legislator making a case to parliament.

"As you know, our Virginia is perhaps the most vibrant and prosperous of all the British colonies. Cotton and tobacco from Southern colonies are in great demand worldwide. Our year-round climate is ideal for producing great quantities for export while providing an idyllic location for our colonial life. Chesapeake Bay is also proving to be one of the finest fishing grounds in the world."

"William," Helen interrupted, "you speak as if making a speech. These are all things of which I am aware."

William held up his hand. "Yes, certainly, my dear. I beg your continued indulgence." William took a deep breath and exhaled slowly. With a slight smile, he continued, "The English are not the only ones to see the enormous value of Virginia and the surrounding frontier. The French have been sending incursions into the nearby Ohio River Valley, an area claimed by our Virginia Colony. Our governor, Willem Anne van Keppel, second Earl of Albemarle, has become alarmed. He has received a string of reports highlighting Indian attacks and continued French activity in the region. Though it would be nice if our governor would visit his colony on occasion, he now relies on our friend Robert Dinwiddie to govern the colony in his absence. Dinwiddie is de facto head of the colony, and we might hope that he will be rightfully appointed as lieutenant governor one day.

"The earl has applied pressure on Mr. Dinwiddie to secure the region, and in his most recent communication, he expressed doubts as to Robert's ability to do so. Now, as you know, Robert has successfully negotiated the Treaty of Lancaster, deeding the land of Virginia to the British from the Iroquois Indians. A survey team has marked the boundaries, and the Indians have agreed. It is a major success for our own Robert Dinwiddie.

"As you also know, the survey team included my contemporary, Major George Washington. Dinwiddie has been relying heavily on Washington's support in the effort with the Indians."

Young William was becoming restless in Helen's arms, and she interjected, "William, I really hate to act impatient, but I know all of this. How does this involve you?"

"I will bring this all to a conclusion," William promised. "Robert is now anxious to send a strong message back to the governor and his king that they can put their complete trust in him. He cannot afford to leave the colony, so he must send an emissary with the great news of the land purchase. Along with the news, he will send a large gift of silver and gold, collected from the colonists, to remind the governor and his king of how prosperous the colony would be under Dinwiddie's leadership.

"The question now is: Who can he trust to send as his representative? His first choice would obviously be Washington, yet he will need the young major to secure the land along the Ohio River from the French."

Helen now smiled. "And the obvious next best choice to convey the message would be the young and handsome Adjunct General William Tanner."

William simply said, "Precisely."

Helen was reminded then why her husband was so special. William was a handsome and intelligent man, held in high regard by the colonials, as well as with those who represented the king. He was honest beyond reproach and devout in his Christian convictions. She had heard others say that he was destined for great things. His gentlemanly charm was representative of the best that the Southern colonies had to offer.

"Yes," William agreed, "I certainly could not reject such an assignment. My only request of Robert, however, was that I be able to travel with my beautiful wife and brilliant son. I explained that other than my God and Savior, there is nothing dearer to me in this world. I cannot stand the thought of being without them for the months it will take to finish the task. Robert consented, and we have already begun the preparations for the trip." He paused briefly and then asked,

"Certainly, I made it clear that your consent was required. Do I have your consent, my dear?"

Helen could see that William was hopeful she would share his excitement. His career was going well, and he was obviously confident that he could convince the governor and the king that the colonials had things well in hand. This could certainly be a stage from which he could spring forth to even better and more brilliant opportunities. He really didn't need to ask, for she would go anywhere he went. But she loved him for his show of respect for what was important to her.

Instead of directly answering her husband, Helen's mind raced through all the details for their preparation to depart. She announced, "We must contact the Jefferson family. I do hope that Jane Randolph will be able to stand in for me at the home while we are away."

Helen and a small group of like-minded women organized, operated, and served at a home that cared for the neediest and most outcast children in the colony. These children were either severely disfigured or damaged, with broken hearts and minds—orphaned by parents due to their death or inability to cope. Helen was attracted to those who were the most rejected by society. Her gift was to see beyond their ghastly features or offensive behavior and love them unconditionally.

Her husband often wished that his wife would seek other endeavors, but he had to admit that she was right, and he loved her that much more for it.

Helen sheepishly looked over to young William and, with sadness, remarked, "Mrs. Jefferson will be so sorry to hear that her son Thomas will be losing his close playmate for so long."

Helen then called for their black housekeeper, Auntie Babe, and began reciting all the things she was going to need to prepare for their trip.

In the midst of her recitation, William interjected, "We shall have only a matter of days to ready ourselves for our departure. The next of the king's ships to set sail from York for England is the man-of-war

HMS *Royal Countenance*. I am certain she'll be anxious to deliver her cargo of colonial silver and gold to the king and will not wait for us."

Chapter Fourteen

Captain Giddy Gilcox stood at the helm on the quarterdeck of the *Rogue Flattery* as she plowed north along the coast. He cringed as he saw the Greek approaching him from the ship's waist. Giddy had to remind himself that it was necessary he give this sailor the impression that he'd welcomed him into his confidence.

The truth was that Giddy was growing to detest the Greek's arrogant impertinence more each day. He had witnessed his openly trying to gain favor with the crew and soliciting their allegiance in preparation for taking over the ship. He needed the Greek for his future plans, however, so he let him live.

Niko approached the captain with an informality that none of the other crew enjoyed. "Ah, my captain, who will we rob, steal from, or kill today, eh? We do much of that but not much to show for it, eh?"

At that moment, Giddy would have sliced any other man's throat, but he took a deep breath and replied, "Mr. Niko, we must never lose our edge. Much bigger prizes await, I assure you. My Greek friend, you have proven to be a ruthless and bloodthirsty pirate—a fine addition to our crew."

The quartermaster Chauncy Cortlaroy passed on deck beneath Gilcox and the Greek as they spoke. The two watched as Cortlaroy poked his index finger into the underarm of another sailor who was in the middle of reaching high up to pull rigging taut.

The man yelped in pain and jumped back, letting go of the line. He immediately turned to retaliate but noticing it was Cortlaroy, he stopped and halfheartedly laughed as he rubbed his armpit. Cortlaroy smiled a devilish smile back at the man and continued on.

Niko spoke up to the captain, "I do not like that queer man. He act like girl, and he cause trouble with crew. Why do they not kill him? If he do that to me, I will kill him."

"Mr. Niko, that man is Chauncy Cortlaroy. He is my quartermaster, and he is very good at what he does."

Niko quickly responded, "He may be good, but he cause trouble with men. I warn you, Captain, if he touch me, I will cut him to pieces."

"Well, my fine Greek friend, I want you to live beyond today, so I will give you fair warning. Do not enter into a duel with our quartermaster. I assure you, he will have his way with you."

Other than Gilcox, Cortlaroy was the most merciless and deadly swordsman on the ship. His manner was deceiving, as he was a tall, thin, and slightly built man with an artistic nature. Cortlaroy was certainly not a natural sailor but a landlubber who chose exile to the sea rather than the sure penalty of his heinous crimes on land.

For years, Chauncy Cortlaroy flitted about in British social circles that included the highest of society and even some of the extended royal family. He fancied himself an actor, which proved to be true in that he was able to gain favor with those who would normally shun persons of his background and lineage.

It wasn't until the king's guard began closing in on the suspect of the brutal murders of young society ladies that Cortlaroy donned the dirty clothes, the crude demeanor, and the harsh accent of a mariner—and then faked his way onto one of the Gilcox ships. Giddy was on that voyage and saw right through his act, yet he was impressed with

Cortlaroy's intelligence and keen skills at requisitioning, ciphering numbers, and organization. Giddy also found Chauncy's quick wit and sharper tongue entertaining. He would talk circles around the crew and even the officers.

Gilcox maintained contact with Cortlaroy for several years after that first voyage to make use of his talents. When Giddy was preparing to abscond with the *Rogue Flattery*, he hired on Chauncy Cortlaroy to outfit and supply her for her future in sea piracy.

The Greek commented, "Captain, I don't care if he is king of England; you tell him to stay away from Niko, or I swear you will need another quartermaster."

Gilcox concealed his disgust for Niko and said, "I have already had words with Mr. Cortlaroy to hold his tongue about you. I assure you, though, he has no fear of you. On this ship, Cortlaroy cares for no one but himself. He rightfully fears his captain and resentfully respects Mr. Blackbury's strength and reliability, but the rest of the crew, including yourself, he loathes."

"Why he hate me?" Niko was offended and growing angry. "I do nothing to him. What could he say about Niko?"

The captain was happy to reply. "Well, except for the fact that you are dirty and smell like a dead animal, he simply cares very little for you."

Cortlaroy was a stickler for cleanliness. He would bathe four times a day if Gilcox would let him. The quartermaster enjoyed fine, frilly clothes and would don pungent perfumes.

The Greek continued to glare at Cortlaroy from a distance and answered, "I hear the men call him the name, Chauncy Chutney. I think it mean he is crazy."

"No, Mr. Niko, the nickname 'Chutney' comes from the thick, sweet, and bitter jam you will see him smother on everything he eats. It is also an excellent description of Cortlaroy. His outward appearance is refined and his speech flowery, while underneath is a bitter, vicious, and cruel man."

"What would happen if I call that name to his face?"

"All I can say is that the first two men who tried were made into mincemeat in a sword duel. Neither survived their wounds, but Chauncy was left without a scratch. My crew learned that despite his frail features, he is a quick and deadly swordsman. He was trained by some of the finest swordsmen in England."

Niko probed further. "If no one like him, then why they not all jump him and kill him?"

"Well, I presume it's because his verbal scorchings provide entertainment for all but the one being torched. Everyone, with the exception of myself, has been roasted at one time or another."

Gilcox himself wondered when the crew might rise up to deal with Cortlaroy's irritating antics, his provoking the men for the pure entertainment of his swordplay, but they all had learned to accept the bruise, laugh it off, and swallow their pride. Also, the fact that their captain would be angered by the loss of a valued quartermaster had something to do with their acceptance of Cortlaroy's treatment.

"If he hate all these men," Niko asked, "then why do he stay on this ship?"

"Well, my hairy Greek friend, the fact of the matter is that none of the crew can stop being one of the *Rogue Flattery* without my permission. I promised Cortlaroy that one day, we would touch the shores of Europe, and only then would I cut him loose. He has no other choice but to bide his time and wait."

The Greek reiterated his original point. "Well, you tell that man to keep away from Niko. I not afraid of him. If he touch me or say something about me, we will see who is quickest with sword."

Gilcox was growing weary of the Greek's company. He looked southeast and spotted a British man-of-war on the horizon. He concluded the conversation. "That will be enough, Mr. Niko. I have already warned Cortlaroy to keep his distance from you. Rest assured, you are a big part of my future plans. Now, please move to your station."

The Greek spotted what Gilcox was looking at in the distance, and he grinned as he moved away. "Yes, my captain. Another ship for us to take?"

Gilcox called out, "Mr. Blackbury to the quarterdeck!"

As Niko passed through the men, the word quickly spread, and the crew started to mobilize for a fight, anticipating a call to quarters.

The entire crew reacted with surprise and disappointment when they heard Gilcox order, "Continue our course north by northeast. Full and bye, Mr. Blackbury, full and bye."

Chapter Fifteen

Before long, the *Rogue Flattery* had left the fighting ship in her distant wake.

Blackbury walked up to the captain and said, "The men are surprised, Cap'n. They nevah seen us run from a fight before."

"No, soldier," Gilcox angrily answered, "I never have, and I never will. It doesn't shock me that these nitwits are surprised. I'll do all the thinking that is necessary on this ship. There is a plan, and I will see it through, even though it may appear we are running from a fight. We run only because I desire to be chased. As you know, we have been sailing deliberately slowly. I would expect it would have allowed sufficient time for our adversary, the good officer Christian, to move ahead of us to Virginia. If that ship is the HMS *Sovereign*, then I am appalled at how slow they are to achieve their destination. If it isn't the *Sovereign*, then I don't care to risk a tussle before I put my plan into effect." The captain paused and took a deep breath while facing into the wind. "Mr. Blackbury, please take command. Continue heading north by northeast off the coast. I shall retire to my cabin, and I do not wish to be disturbed."

The pirates continued their tack beyond their destination, intending to circle back to Virginia to make certain that Christian was at anchor when their real target was set to sail.

~~~

Gilcox sat in his cabin, thinking through every detail of his escape plan. Questions hung in his mind, as he was beginning to wonder if he had misjudged or overestimated the capability of his pursuer. The plan involved avoiding confrontation with Christian until Gilcox built up significant wealth and then identified just the right ship to replace his beloved *Rogue Flattery*. Though it pained him to give up his mistress, he knew there was growing knowledge of her. He also knew she was now recognizable by her distinct design and had become very much the "hunted". Gilcox had been preparing himself for the day when a growing level of knowledge about her would require a new start.

His plan was to sail north, bury their treasure somewhere safe, then seize a replacement ship and hide her away. He would set the *Rogue Flattery* in a place where even a blind sailor could not miss her. The Greek had proven to be a troublemaker with a taste for mutiny. Gilcox would use this to his advantage, as a number of Giddy's most trusted men would coax the Greek into leading them in a feigned mutiny to oust their captain and his officers. The mutineers would lock Gilcox and most of the pirates in one hold, and the other most dimwitted pirates in another hold.

In the dark of night, the trusted pirates would murder the Greek, making it sound as though they had killed Gilcox. The dimwits would then hear the mutineers, one by one, dragging the officers and the men from the other hold topside to convince them to join the mutiny. When they refused, each would appear to be noisily executed and thrown overboard.

In reality, Gilcox and his most loyal crew members would steal away, leaving the dimwits waiting their turn. Only Sachumjuia would remain until the Royal Navy closed in on the *Rogue Flattery*. The Indian would then release the dimwits to fight the navy, claiming he had killed the mutineers. As they scurried to set off a few rounds at the British man-of-war, the Indian would light a fuse to a charge that would sink the *Rogue Flattery* in full sight of the navy as he slipped away for his long swim back to Gilcox and his remaining crew.

Giddy expected there would be a few survivors from the dimwits who would give a full account of all that transpired. Then, being the only ones left who could possibly identify Gilcox, the dimwits would be ceremoniously hanged by the Royal Navy, leaving Gilcox and the remaining crew with a whole new start.

Giddy grimaced as he pondered the one flaw in his own plan—a flaw that was found within himself. Could he ever find an adequate replacement for his precious *Rogue Flattery*? He believed he was willing to give her up, but there was not a ship on the open sea that could live up to the standards set in her creator's mind. With each ship they came upon, even those that were quite serviceable, he would find some fault he could not accept.

Only the officers knew of their captain's plan, and he could see their frustration. Even though they would encourage him that a particular ship was adequate, he would reject each one out of hand. Would this fickleness be his plan's undoing?

The last decent prospect had been the Spanish slave ship. He didn't like to think about that ship, but it kept coming to his mind. With every memory, he would feel an eerie sensation overcome him. He wondered if the evil hadn't moved over from the Spanish vessel to visit his own ship. Perhaps it was time to let the *Rogue Flattery* go, and maybe that would put an end to this cursed feeling. He shook off the oppressive feelings and left his cabin to go topside.

After sailing farther north beyond the mouth of the York River, Blackbury found a hidden spot within the intercoastals where they could lie in wait. The *Rogue Flattery* was put to anchor, and a longboat was outfitted with a mast and sails. Captain Gilcox gave orders for his first mate, along with two crewmen, to set sail for York to uncover the details regarding the king's ship and her departure plans. He wanted to gauge how strong her defenses were and see if Christian's ship was anywhere to be found.

Chapter Sixteen

In Williamsburg, Helen Tanner was busily finishing her packing and organizing the final arrangements. Auntie Babe was softly weeping as she put the final touches on all the packing. Helen was struggling to console her while fighting back her own tears. She could hear a growing commotion coming closer to the back door. Helen hurried outside, with Auntie Babe following behind.

Helen found Babe's twelve-year-old son, Leroy, crying and carrying little William toward the house. William was also crying, and blood flowed from a wound on his forehead. Leroy's father, old Uncle Jubalee, followed behind, scolding Leroy and slapping him on the side of his head.

Helen maintained her calm but called, "My, my, you boys hurry inside. We'll clean that up and you'll be fine, William. Babe, go retrieve a pan of water and a cloth."

Helen took young William from Leroy's arms and comforted her little boy by kissing the top of his head and caressing his cheeks. William snuggled to her breast with his hands clasped around her soft white nape. Immediately, he calmed down—he was nestled in his greatest place of comfort. Looking down as she ran her fingers through his hair, Helen could tell that he was listening to the beating of her heart. *It must be much the same as the sense of comfort that he knew in my womb.*

She began to sweetly sing his favorite hymns as she watched him stare at the glistening gold cross that always hung from her neck. It was his plaything that would mesmerize him and take his mind off of his hurts. It seemed to bring him a comfort that reached down all the way from heaven.

Taking the wet cloth from Babe, Helen carefully wiped the boy's forehead, and then turned to Babe's son. "Now tell me, Leroy, what on earth happened?"

Leroy apprehensively looked at his father as he carefully answered. "Me and William been playin' sword fightin' wid sticks. The play gots a little excited, and I thinks William's gonna duck, but he don't. The stick hits him wid a loud smack. We both stands there lookin' at each other, and I think it be all fine. William be startin' ta laugh when he felt the blood come down his face. I wants ta run 'cause I knows dis mean a beatin', but I cain't. I feels so bad for our little William. I loves dat boy so I picks him up and carries him home."

As Leroy told the story, Helen looked over at old Uncle Jubalee, sitting in the corner. She could tell that his anger was boiling up as he mumbled, "Lazy...no good...gots no business..."

Leroy had just finished saying, "I's sorry," when his father jumped up to slap him again.

"No!" young William screamed. "Don't hurt him!"

With that, Helen jumped in. "Jubalee! That will be enough. Boys will be boys. Leroy would never try to hurt William. We won't have another word about it!"

With that, old Jubalee got up and excused himself. "Miss Helen, ma'am, Jubalee's feelin' a bit uneasy. I fears that somebody's done goin' ta pay a price for all dis."

Helen tried to reassure him. "Jubalee, don't you worry about this.

You know the Tanners aren't like old Tom. There will be no more about this matter." She knew he would have a hard time believing her. Helen quietly rocked in her chair to calm William, and she felt sad as she thought of the hard life her slaves had led prior to joining their family...

Old Uncle Jubalee, his wife, Babe (twenty years his junior), and his boy, Leroy, had been with the Tanners for almost six years. William Sr. purchased them shortly before his marriage to Helen. Babe had shared with Helen what their life was like in Charlottesville when they were owned by an old mountain man named Tom, who abused them all terribly.

According to Babe, the man got himself stone drunk one night and walked off a cliff. Though they were used to the man disappearing and then suddenly reappearing, this had seemed the longest he had ever been away. The black slaves kept busy until one day, weeks later, when the constable came and told them of the man's death.

Babe had recalled fondly how much they enjoyed their time alone up on old Tom's mountain and how much it felt like playtime for them. Acting as if they were free persons, for a fleeting moment they thought that maybe life could go on like that. However, they were eventually informed that they would be sold to pay off the mountain man's debts.

Fortunately for them, the constable was an acquaintance of a young William Tanner and knew he was looking for slaves to run property he had just purchased. The arrangements were made, and old Jubalee and his family quickly learned that things would be different under their new master.

Jubalee had to actually train William on how to manage his slaves, as it was obvious that the new owner had no knowledge of these things and was much too lenient. Babe and Leroy were both just glad for the new start, with the raw treatment of the past left behind them up on Tom's mountain. Old Jubalee still stayed fearful that the next beating was somehow around the corner. No matter how much better things were, he acted certain that some terrible treatment would be visited upon them.

Helen looked down lovingly at her son. For little William, they were all his family. They had been a part of his life since he was born. He had just started to notice the physical differences, but the blacks were still his family—a family of six, with Auntie Babe as much a mother to him as his own; Jubalee, his crotchety old uncle; and Leroy, his brother and best friend.

The fact was, he spent more time with them than he did with his busy mother and father. Recently, William had asked, "Mum, why does Father speak differently to Aunt and Uncle and Leroy? Doesn't he love them?"

Helen's heart sank with the realization that William was beginning to comprehend the difference between slave and owner. She chose her words carefully, "No, no. Your father loves them, too. He just loves us that much more." Helen hoped she was showing her son, by example, that she loved them all as family.

Suddenly, Auntie Babe broke down in tears. "Why can't we go wid ya ta England?"

"Now, Auntie Babe," Helen sadly answered, "I have been through this many times already. We have tried to arrange for all of us to go on the trip, but that just won't be possible. It breaks my heart, but Master William, being on the Crown's business, is being allowed passage on the Royal Navy vessel, HMS *Royal Countenance*. The ship is enormous, but it's not built for many passengers. They simply will not allow any more than Master William and his immediate family."

"Please, Miss Helen," Auntie Babe pleaded, "we his family. I'll stay anywheres, in any crack or hole. Dey never knows we's there."

"Babe, for this voyage, extra soldiers will be on board, due to the valuable cargo. I've shed my own tears to William, but there simply isn't room. I'm so, so sorry."

Helen looked over at Jubalee and caught him smiling. She knew that although Babe and Leroy were heartbroken, old Uncle Jubalee likely was looking forward to feeling like a free man and master of the house for the months while the Tanners were away.

Chapter Seventeen

Lieutenant Commander Leslie Christian sat in the captain's quarters of the HMS *Sovereign* as the ship sailed north to engage the pirates at sea. There came a knock on his door to which he responded, "Enter."

Lieutenant Wilson came in and saluted. "Sir, reporting that we are running at full sail with a strong wind off our stern. We shall make good time now, sir."

Christian pushed back from his desk. "Yes, I am pleased with our progress. We made our necessary preparations in Jamaica in a timely manner, as we did not have the marines to contend with, nor did our crew have the fear of Albatross to hinder us this time."

"Yes, sir," Wilson agreed. "And adding a few more guns and more seasoned sailors to our arsenal took some time, but I believe you have effectively persuaded the men that we have the pirates on the run. I detect that our crew has much greater confidence they can defeat these pirates at sea."

"And by God, we shall, Mr. Wilson; we shall. We certainly know we are on their trail. The evidence of the pirates' doings is like a trail of bread crumbs left to lead us to them. These pirates don't appear to show any particular discernment or discrimination regarding the ships they scuttle, no matter their size or potential reward."

"No, sir," Wilson said. "They have left in their wake the debris from cargo ships, barges, baroques, sloops, cutters, ferries, bumboats, gigs, schooners, snows, brigs—almost every floating vessel imaginable. I would imagine that there were few valuables found on many of these ships, other than stores to replenish their supplies. I swear, sir, it is almost as if you can hear the echoed cries of the poor desperate sailors they murder. And we also have evidence that, at least twice, they went ashore to engage in village raids near the ports of St. Augustine and, now, Savannah."

Christian shook his head. He had been reading as much as he could about the famous Caribbean pirates and about Gilcox himself. He'd spent hours trying to understand who these men were and what made them so evil.

Almost as an echo to Christian's thoughts, Fulton asked, "Sir, what causes men to become what they become? What makes them decide to become pirates?"

"Mr. Wilson, I have asked myself that very question. I have tried to put myself in their minds but have found it impossible. This pirate captain and his crew are more like a mad shiver of sharks than human beings. I have asked myself, how is it that death and destruction can come so easily to a whole ship of men? How can the laws of man and God be so easily disregarded without any inkling of guilt apparent among them? I have made a study of these men, and there is some commonality. Giddy Gilcox and—to a degree—all the others share a common interest: all have been buried at the bottom of the class system. Whether it is due to physical rejection, social ostracism, or legal restraint, each has likely been abused, neglected, and shown little mercy with their lot in life."

Wilson shook his head. "Does that give them license to perpetrate evil onto others?"

"No, of course not," Christian was quick to answer. "But for men who love the freedom of life on the sea, piracy offers them the chance to rise above their dreary lot and gain some control over their own destiny. It provides a chance to enjoy wealth and freedom that they would never have achieved by following the path that was predestined for them."

Wilson was drawn into the ring of truth in his captain's words. "But why to such excess?"

"The evil consumes these men," Christian responded. "To maintain freedom and wealth, Gilcox and the others have determined that blood will have to be shed. Not just a little but a lot."

"Such evil and disregard for humanity? It is hard to comprehend."

"As I understand it," the commander concluded, "the desire to strive for greater freedom is natural to man. Yet that same desire, for these men, has grown into a need to become master of all. The pirates feel they are now the conquerors, and the same lack of mercy that was shown to them will be dispensed in spades to anyone who stands between them and their desires. Whatever has been destined not to be theirs will now become theirs for the taking. Others' lives now have little value, other than to provide exercises for the pirates to prove themselves as masters over all, particularly over those who, in the past, would have never given them a second thought."

Both men shook their heads and remained quietly in thought. The silence was broken by the sound of the ship bell. Christian could hear orders being given and men running on deck. There was a knock as the door opened and the first mate entered, excitedly announcing, "Sir, we've spotted a strange ship on the horizon directly off our bow."

The commander jumped up and ran with Wilson to the quarterdeck. The first mate handed the captain his spyglass.

"Hello," Christian muttered as he surveyed the horizon. "I believe I have my first glimpse of the pirate ship *Rogue Flattery*. Take a look, Mr. Wilson." He handed the spyglass to Wilson, saying, "I would prefer not to engage the pirates right now, but we must call the men to quarters to prepare for a fight. We shall not chase them, but if they want to have a go of it, the *Sovereign* will be ready."

Christian was well aware of the reports of the pirate ship's sleek appearance, great stealth, and speed. As soon as he laid eyes on her, he was certain that it was Gilcox's ship.

Wilson gazed through the spyglass. "Sir, it appears that the pirates have hauled their brace lines to a sharp tack and are quickly putting distance between themselves and the *Sovereign*. She's on the run, sir."

"Very well, Mr. Wilson. We shall not chase them, but we must make Virginia with haste."

Christian was excited. Seeing the pirates turn and run gave him even greater confidence that the pirates feared and respected their adversary. He had his own plan to capture the pirates, but he needed to get to Virginia before them.

Chapter Eighteen

The *Sovereign* sailed up the York River and anchored just meters from the *Royal Countenance*. Christian breathed a sigh of relief when he first saw the ship, for he knew when she was scheduled to depart. Numerous circumstances might have arisen to send the *Royal Countenance* home early or to make the *Sovereign* late for the rendezvous.

Christian called for Wilson. When the lieutenant arrived, Christian said, "Please arrange for a meeting with Lieutenant Commander Christopher Wayneright, captain of the *Royal Countenance*."

"Shall I request that he come meet on board the *Sovereign*? And for what time, sir?"

"No, we will go to him, and we'll do so immediately," Christian responded. "You will find that the man is not only rotund but is as pompous and arrogant as the size of his belly. Wayneright was my junior, graduating from a naval class a year behind mine. I had met him on several occasions and found him very difficult. He didn't seem to care for me, and now that I have been commissioned on this notable assignment, I'm sure he is quite jealous."

When Christian arrived at the captain's quarters on board the *Royal Countenance*, he was not surprised to find that Wayneright was openly displeased. The two men struggled through an exchange of formal courtesies.

They stood in awkward silence for a moment until Wayneright, laying all friendly pretenses aside, interjected, "Christian, we are on an extremely tight schedule. We will be leaving on the morrow with a robust load of royal cargo that His Majesty is quite anxious to receive. I still have preparations to make; please state your true purpose."

Christian had fully expected this pompous attitude and was ready with his response. "My purpose, sir, is to ensure that your cargo gets into the hands of its rightful owner, the king. We have followed the pirate Giddy Gilcox north and know he is in these waters. We have information from a reliable source that he intends to scuttle your ship."

Wayneright seemed preoccupied and disinterested. He waited for Christian to finish speaking and then retorted, "Preposterous! A pirate dog plunder one of the finest ships and crews in the king's navy? I question your reasoning skills, sir! And if this fantasy is true, I relish the thought of the engagement. It will be but a source of entertainment to break up the long voyage home."

Again, Christian had expected such a response from Wayneright. However, he nodded in agreement, saying, "Most certainly, commander. I have full confidence that the *Royal Countenance* would prove victorious, but I don't believe we should take any chances with the king's property. My royal charge is to capture and hang these pirates, and I only ask that we work together to ensure victory. Gilcox has a formidable ship, and your support in apprehending the pirates would mean much more to the king than merely delivering cargo."

Wayneright visibly bristled. "How dare you! Do I appear to you as fish bait?"

"Support me in this effort," Christian cut in, "and I will make certain you receive a full measure of the glory." With that, he quietly sat back and watched Wayneright as the rotund officer pondered his proposal. *He knows I am right. His assignment to transport the king's property back and forth to the Americas will never lead to a higher commission. Moreover, if he should ever lose any of the cargo, his career would be finished.*

Wayneright leaned forward. "Agreed. I shall need to strengthen my arsenal and add a few more men. I expect that we shall sail as planned, keeping a watchful eye and tarrying a bit to ensure that your *Sovereign* is not too far behind, if and when the pirates attack."

"As for the *Sovereign*," Christian countered, "she will immediately sail up and around a bend in the York River to anchor where she can keep the *Royal Countenance* in sight from her crow's nest. Around daybreak, when all your hands are assembled, you will fire a shot from your cannon as a signal for your departure. The *Sovereign* will weigh anchor one hour later. If there are any major delays, a messenger will be sent for any updates. Are we agreed?"

"Agreed, Commander," Wayneright responded. "Nothing short of a hurricane will stop the *Royal Countenance* from her appointed departure. We will be departing sharply at six bells." Wayneright stood, signaling the end of the meeting. He paused, as if suddenly remembering something, then said, "I have a colonial official and his family on board. Do you think I should require them to make other arrangements?" Before Christian could respond, however, Wayneright answered his own question. "No, no, I am confident that if anything should transpire, our advance notice will assure that we shall swiftly sink the pirates without any close contact. They shall be safe under my care. Certainly, what better praise could there be of the *Royal Countenance*'s capability than that of a civilian official grateful for our protection?"

Wayneright's mood had greatly improved since the beginning of their conversation, and he picked up a crystal decanter. "Would you like to join me in a glass of brandy to toast our certain victory, Christian?"

"No, I'm sorry, Captain," Christian answered, "but I must be going. There is still much I must attend to."

"Well, I, for one, will enjoy several glasses to ensure a good night's sleep so as to be well rested for tomorrow."

The two naval officers saluted and shook hands. As Christian was leaving, he stopped at the door to pass along one last thought. "I would suggest we not share our plan with anyone other than our senior officers. If the pirates are monitoring our activity, then any change in plans might signal them to change theirs."

As Christian departed, he felt an exhilaration and excitement for the certain victory that lay ahead. He could almost taste the powder in the air.

His excitement began to wane, though, as it dawned on him that Wayneright might try to steal a quick victory on his own to take the full credit. He was aware that Wayneright had yet to experience the thrill of battle at sea. The rotund captain was sure to see this as his opportunity to heroically shine.

When Christian returned to the *Sovereign*, he pulled Wilson aside. "Place a lookout in the *Sovereign*'s crow's nest this evening with orders to confirm by sight when the *Royal Countenance* departs. The departure is not scheduled until after daybreak, but I expect to hear reports at each bell throughout the evening."

"Very well, sir," Wilson responded, "but is that really necessary? It will be a cool, damp evening with almost no visibility as a result of a heavy fog that's rolling in. Is a lookout necessary, given the fact that the *Royal Countenance* is planning to fire a gun as a signal when she departs?"

"I know it seems excessive, but I don't want to leave anything to chance with Gilcox, and I don't particularly trust our fat friend."

~~~

Over on the *Royal Countenance*, as was required, the lieutenant governor and his family were all stowed away in their cabin for the evening. Civilians would not be a cause for any delay, but a last night of shore leave for the sailors would end at four in the morning, with dire consequences for those who were not assembled to be ferried out to the ship.

Young William Tanner was overwhelmed by all the activity. Along with innumerable farewells, there had been a whirlwind of last-minute details to contend with. Many people from the community came out to see them off. He wished his auntie Babe could have been there, but she was sick and had to stay home. William heard her tell his mother that she had very bad feelings about their trip. These feelings made her so sick that she was put to bed. His mother had tried to assure Auntie Babe that the family was squarely within God's hands and that, God willing, they would all return home safely. This did little to comfort his auntie.

Young William, on the other hand, was particularly impressed with how much attention his father was given. It was obvious, even to this five-year-old, that his father was well respected and beloved. His father, in turn, handled himself in a self-assured and stately manner. Whatever his mission was, it seemed that all of Virginia had confidence in his father to carry it out.

Then there was the ship. William Jr. was overwhelmed by the size and stature of the ship and all her glistening black guns. The immensity of everything intimidated him, but still, he wanted desperately to explore every inch of her. William Jr. was particularly frustrated and angry when he was required to go to sleep as soon as the family was settled in their cabin.

Falling asleep was a struggle, but eventually, he dropped off, only to awaken some time later to the soft rocking of the ship. It was completely dark, save for a faint light coming through a porthole. Raising himself up, he peered out into the darkness. Through a brief break in the fog, William saw a man with a raised lantern on the shore, which the ship slowly slid past. William jumped down and scampered over to his father's berth. "Father, our ship is sailing!"

His father opened his sleepy eyes and briefly smiled. "Certainly, son. We shall not stop until we see the king's castle. Now go back to your bed and sleep."

William did as he was told, but he could not contain his excitement for all that would come with the morning light.

Chapter Nineteen

Lieutenant Commander Christian was up early to make certain everything was ready to sail at the appointed time. The latest call up to the crow's nest brought the familiar response, "All's well!" The fog continued to be as thick as smoke, so Christian had a mind to lower a boat to make physical contact with the *Royal Countenance*.

Suddenly, a boat filled with sailors emerged from the fog. First Mate Wilson was about to call men to quarters to brace for an attack when the captain intervened.

"Identify yourself and state your purpose!" the captain called down to the men in the boat.

A voice came back, "We're the crew of the *Royal Countenance*, come to report our situation."

Christian thought it odd to send so many men for a report but replied, "Very well; come aboard."

The voice hesitated but then called back, "Sir, I don't believe we have time. She's gone!"

Christian was confused. "Who's gone? Tell me directly!"

The voice nervously confessed, "The HMS *Royal Countenance* has disappeared, and we cannot find her. Almost all of the crew has been left behind!"

Christian's confusion suddenly became clear. It was as though someone had screamed the answer into his ear. *Gilcox!*

With a roar, he called his men to quarters, and as quickly as they had ever accomplished, they weighed anchor. Under full sail, they swiftly navigated the channel of the York River, racing to reach open water. This was very risky with the heavy fog, and they were fortunate that the only resulting damage was to several other small craft anchored in the river they bumped and swamped.

The fog was just clearing as the ship broke out into open water, but there was no sign of the *Royal Countenance*. Christian was red-faced and enraged. Which direction had they turned? He had to calm down and make a decision. Christian yelled at his first mate, "Set a course due south to follow the coast!"

He prayed to God that he had made the right choice.

~~~

There came a knock on the Captain Gilcox's cabin door, and Giddy responded, "Report."

"Sir," Stroppy Newsome answered from the other side of the door, "we's spotted Blackbury and da reconnaissance party returning."

Giddy went topside and greeted his first mate as he boarded the ship. "What have you found, Mr. Blackbury?"

"Well, sah, I believe I 'ave some valuable information. The king's transport, already loaded wid gold and silver, is set ta sail this next morning. Da port at York is abuzz wid navy sailors sharing every detail ta any dog who'll buy 'em rum an' provide a listening ear."

Giddy probed, "Next morning, eh? What of Christian's ship?"

His first mate was quick to answer. "His ship was also dere but further up da river. Da guards were heavy on shore, but as best we can tell, dere was but a handful ta guard da ship itself. All da rest of da crew is scheduled ta report back from leave at four in da morning. Word is spreading 'at da ship's captain is preparing for an attack, once out ta sea."

Giddy was pleased. "Well done, Mr. Blackbury. We must act quickly."

With this information in hand, Giddy's mind quickly went into action. He gathered his officers together and outlined his plan. "Soldiers, I thought that I might have more time to prepare, but we cannot pass up so fine an opportunity. Mr. Blackbury, you will lead the assault team and utilize our Indian friend as your key weapon. When you sail the longboat back into the harbor, you will determine if the wind, tide, weather, and moon be favorable. If so, you will put my plan into action.

"The Indian will steal aboard the ship, quietly eliminate the guards, and sever the anchor line, setting the ship adrift. Slightly downriver, you and your boat of pirates will join the ship adrift. Some will board her to prepare her to sail, and the rest will take a bow line to slowly and quietly ferry the ship from the port out to the sea. There is much that must go in our favor, but we have the element of surprise on our side. The Royal Navy is under the misunderstanding that pirates are comfortable taking their chances only when in their own element, out on the open sea. I believe this action will never be suspected, and we shall catch the Royal Navy completely off guard. The *Rogue Flattery* will prepare to meet the assault team just south of the mouth of the York River."

~~~

Early the next morning, the longboat sailed into port, and Blackbury sized up the situation. He made the decision to proceed with the plan as the fog rolled in and grew heavier. The fog was so thick that they almost sailed right up to the *Royal Countenance* before seeing her. Immediately, they came about to sail a short distance back downriver to wait for the ship to drift to them. As they came about, Sachumjuia slipped into the water, armed only with a knife and his hatchet. The heavy fog was all they needed to move ahead with their plan.

With the *Royal Countenance* under the pirates' control, they rendezvoused with the *Rogue Flattery*. Even the clever Captain Giddy Gilcox was amazed when he saw the great HMS *Royal Countenance* break through the fog and out into the open water. The two ships immediately sailed south together for a short distance, anchored, and then were secured together with grappling hooks. Giddy and a number of his crew boarded the *Royal Countenance* to survey the pirate Indian's handiwork.

"Sachumjuia," Giddy called out, "can you provide a full report on your action?"

"Aye, I kill each man where standing. No one make any sound."

Giddy was entertained. "Yes, go on. I want to hear your entire action."

"I kill four men on top deck and then go below. I come up to captain's quarters and found captain sleeping. I lock door, knowing Captain Gilcox would want to have fun with British chief."

Giddy resisted a smile but responded, "You thought correctly, my friend. I'll so look forward to this…but please go on."

"I then move to other cabins until I find family sleeping—except for young boy lying in bed. The boy see me, but he not scared. He must think I am part of this crew. I know you want to use them, too, so I tie door shut. With ship secure, I throw tow line to Blackbury and chop anchor lines."

"Well done, my friend," said Giddy, rubbing his hands together, "well done. Let's go below and see your work firsthand. Oh, and yes, I do believe we have some treasure to uncover."

The captain headed below with Sachumjuia, Newsome, and Cortlaroy. As they were coming down the stairs, Giddy heard banging on the captain's door and yelling coming from within the cabin. Wayneright was shouting, "Bloody hell! Who gave orders to sail? Why is this door locked?"

Captain Wayneright suddenly broke through the door, screaming demands to know what was going on. Giddy was amused by the navy captain's air of authority, even as he stood brandishing a sword in his nightshirt. When the officer saw the pirates, he raised his saber and charged them. Giddy calmly raised his flintlock and shot him dead.

The pirate captain looked down at the dead officer and shook his head. "What a shame. This one could have provided some real entertainment."

The pirates moved on to the stateroom with the family inside. Giddy felt certain that this encounter would also prove to be entertaining. He knocked on the door and spoke politely. "This is the captain. May I please enter?"

There was silence for a moment, but then a quivering male voice responded, "Y-yes…you may enter."

The Indian untied the door and pushed it open. Gilcox strolled through the door and saw a couple and a child crouched in the corner. The child had his face pressed against his mother's neck as he grasped tightly to the end of a necklace.

Gilcox's strong and pleasant voice was deceptive, and it always served to make his appearance that much more hideous when he came into view. The man flinched and looked away from the horrible sight. Immediately, Giddy decided his death would be painful. As his anger grew, he glared at the woman, but she stared straight at him, showing no sign of fear. Her reaction was something Gilcox had never experienced, and it caused him to flinch and look down.

The woman not only showed no fear, but she also had a look that he couldn't describe, even as it seemed vaguely familiar. Words like love and compassion and understanding flashed within his mind. He felt confused and asked himself, *What is this strange sensation I am feeling from just one look at this woman?*

Newsome and Cortlaroy, standing outside the cabin door, noticed their captain's strange reaction and glanced quizzically at each other.

The woman spoke to him without a quiver. "Captain, we ask that you not move forward with your dirty deed, but if you must, please complete it and be off. I'm sure that would be best for all involved."

Giddy was speechless. He turned and exited the cabin, stopping in front of the pirates, somewhat dazed.

Newsome spoke up. "Cap'n? What does ya wan' us ta do wid 'em?"

When Giddy did not respond, Cortlaroy asked, "Might I entertain myself with them for a while, Captain?"

Gilcox snapped back into command. "No one will touch them until I say so. Bring the man topside, and take the woman and child over to the *Rogue Flattery* as hostages." He then strode briskly up to the deck to oversee the transfer of silver and gold to his ship.

Chapter Twenty

The *Sovereign* was in full sail, moving at a fast clip, but to her captain, she was crawling. Christian stood on the quarterdeck, peering out, as his hands tightly gripped the cap rail. He wanted to push her faster and faster—with his own strength, if he could. Most of all, he wanted to see some sign of the *Royal Countenance*, but the sea was empty.

He questioned his decision to sail south. His choice was based upon his assumption that Gilcox would head to more familiar waters, but there was no real reason to expect he was going back to a place he appeared to have abandoned. Should they come about and head back north? He was gripped by feelings of helplessness, embarrassment, and anger. He called up to the lookout repeatedly for reports of any ship sightings, but no word came back.

Just when he'd determined to come about and go back to York town to organize a larger search, the lookout cried, "Debris floatin' off da larboard bow!"

The ship began to slow to have a better look. As they came closer, Christian recognized the jetsam as the dead bodies of several sailors and screamed, "Full and bye!"

He was not going to be slowed by anything, now that he knew he was on the pirates' course. He saw the looks of disgust on the faces of some of his crew at their captain's disregard for the fallen sailors and the fact that he couldn't be bothered to fish them from the sea. He might face charges from the admiralty for this breech of sailing etiquette, but there were lives at stake.

"Ship off the starboard bow!" the lookout shouted.

Christian picked up his spyglass and surveyed the coast. There she was: The great ship, with her sails up, was run up onto the beach and rolled to her side, as if she had been heaved down to prepare her for cleaning. They set a course directly for her and, though it seemed hours to the impatient captain, they soon weighed anchor and let a boat down.

Christian and a boarding party rowed to the listing ship—it was difficult to walk upon her deck when they came aboard. Not surprisingly, the ship appeared to be abandoned.

The captain ordered men forward to look for survivors and others aft to look for the gold and silver. Christian surveyed the scene and saw the bloodstains where men had been stationed. His men reported back to him that there was no sign of life or cargo. The reality of the situation hit Christian hard. He struggled to maintain his composure but then cursed under his breath.

One of his men spotted something up in the rigging and pointed to it. "What's 'at, Cap'n?"

A man, bloody and bruised, had been tied to the yardarm, as if he had been crucified. Everything was stripped from him except his trousers. He had several stab wounds to the stomach and chest, and there was blood all over and around him.

As Christian looked closer, he saw that all of the man's fingers and toes had been removed, except for the index finger of his left hand—and it appeared as if the man was pointing due north.

When the men brought him down, they discovered a parchment stuffed into his trouser pocket. Christian opened it and read the following message:

*We have Lieutenant Governor Tanner's
wife and son as hostages. After we are confident you have given up the chase, we will
release them, unharmed, at a secure and safe
location. Their lives are in your hands!*

Christian was flabbergasted. Wayneright's decision not to remove
the family from the *Royal Countenance* had proven to be a deadly
mistake. What should he do now? With every step he took toward
the pirates, the picture grew uglier and uglier. He leaned back on the
bulwark and stared at the deck. The crew was milling about, waiting
for their orders. Once again, Christian rose up, determined that he
would not let this lying, thieving murderer get away.

First, Christian knew that Gilcox was a notorious liar. He decided
that the hostages were probably dead already, so he would not let that
impede his mission. Second, he decided that because the deceiving
pirate had arranged the man's finger to point north, it must be a false
clue.

The captain authoritatively barked out orders. "All right, men, let
us return to the ship, posthaste. We have no time to lose. We must set
a course due south, for we have pirates to hang!"

The men cheered as they returned to the *Sovereign* to roust the
pirate scoundrels from their Caribbean waters.

Chapter Twenty One

Captain Giddy Gilcox had become so disillusioned with the capability of his adversary that he was determined not to give him any more credit as a sailor and ship captain than he felt Christian deserved. To make certain of meeting up with Christian, Gilcox had left two clues he was certain the Royal Navy captain would follow. The first was the hostage note; no self-respecting gentleman naval officer would dare shrink from rescuing women and children. The second clue was arranging for the husband, as his last dying act, to point north, showing the way to his family's captors. Could Christian possibly miss these clues?

Giddy now had a sense of Christian's sailing speed and calculated that he would have a good week to arrange his plan before Christian could catch up to the pirate ship.

The *Rogue Flattery* was galloping at a breakneck pace under full sail, with a tremendous wind directly off her stern. She raced north along the colonial coast, headed toward Narragansett Bay. Most of the crew had only been this far north in the Americas once, when they had escaped from England years earlier. They were headed to Sachum-juia's home waters, near the place known as Cape Cod. There would be plenty of shipping from which to choose a replacement vessel to complete Giddy's plan.

The captain called for his officers, along with the Mohegan, to join him in his quarters. Giddy rolled out a map of the Connecticut, Rhode Island, and Providence plantations and the Massachusetts Bay Colony coasts on his desk.

The Indian never offered much to say, but he understood perfectly when Giddy asked, "Mr. Sachumjuia, can you identify shipping lanes, safe places to anchor, and locations where we might go ashore, if necessary?"

Sachumjuia silently pointed out the locations.

"I believe," Gilcox instructed his men, "that operating in these northern waters, while offering great opportunities, also adds great risk. More specifically, Mr. Sachumjuia, could you identify a safe and secluded place where we might offload our treasure? It will only be for a short time, but we must have a place where we can quickly come and go without being discovered until my plan is completed."

Throughout his years as a sailor of fortune, there was hardly a shred of evidence to connect him and his pirates to any of their terrible deeds. Giddy's attention to detail made sure of it. Now, if they were going to run into trouble, he did not want any of the freshly stolen booty to be on board until they were ready to escape across the ocean. Once they had hidden the treasure, Gilcox could complete his plan, and they could then dispose of the only other evidence of their pirating: the woman and child. Until then, the hostages provided some measure of safety, should the navy catch up with them.

Sachumjuia did not hesitate and immediately put his finger down on a small triangle of an island, just a few leagues south of Narragansett Bay.

Gilcox and the others looked at each other, a bit surprised. "You know this island?" Gilcox asked. "You have been there?"

"Yes," Sachumjuia answered, "but only one time. The island is called Manisses. My people know it well. Our tribe fight the island Indians many times. This is place you look for."

An inner sense told Gilcox to be suspicious of the Indian's motives for selecting this island. He asked, "Are there still many inhabitants on the island?"

"No. Island Indians small in number and live with few white fishermen and farmers and their slaves. There no good harbor on this island. This keep many others away. This is place you want," he insisted.

"Any particular danger or risk of which this island presents?"

"I know they hold pirates as prisoners on this island, but if you stay to south end, there is little danger."

Giddy was still suspicious, but he agreed. "It's true. With no good port, it would be that much safer to find an isolated spot to anchor for a short period without being detected. I am confident in our crew's ability and skill at securing the *Rogue Flattery* in the most difficult locations. When it comes time to retrieve the booty, there will be nothing between us and the coast of Europe or Africa." Giddy bent over to look more closely at the map. He put his finger on the small spot. "Mr. Blackbury, set a course directly for the island marked on the map as Block Island."

He excused the men and then thought, *Block Island? I know that name. I have read of this island.* He moved over to the shelves of books, diaries, and ships logs that covered the walls of his cabin. He ran his index finger across the book bindings on one shelf until he came to a particular bound document; he pulled it from the shelf.

The writings were from an English historian, documenting New England coastal properties for the king. Giddy acquired it from a ship the pirates had overtaken six months earlier.

Flipping through the pages of the book, he stopped and began to read...

Block Island

In the year of our Lord 1524, French navigator Verrazzano gave report of the island to Francis I, king of France. The island is located fifty leagues east of New York Harbor, and three leagues from the mainland (latitude 41° 08' north, longitude 71° 33" west). She measures eight miles long by three mile wide, the form being that of a triangle. The navigator named the island *Claudia* and reported, "It was full of hills, covered with trees, well-peopled, for we saw fires all along the coast."

In the year of our Lord 1614, Dutch explorer and trader Adrian Block sailing the yacht *Unrest*, of sixteen tons burthen, explored the coasts of Long Island Sound. While exploring, Block came upon the island, which the inhabitants called Manisses, and named the island for himself: Block Island. He anchored off her coast and viewed the island and the Indians who came to investigate his ship but never set foot upon her soil.

The first explorer to land on the island recorded that despite there being thick forest covering almost the entire island, great quantities of stone and rock were evident everywhere. As to the soil, he documented that he could barely step one foot from another without touching some small "bowlder."

The island Indians, known as the *Manisseans*, appeared to be friendly to the English, peacefully harvesting clams and oysters and growing much corn. One day, while an English trader named Oldham visited the island, the Indians killed him and his crew and stole all his belongings. When his ship was discovered by the English authorities, an expedition, under the command of Col. John Endicot, was dispatched to the island. Many Indians were killed, their camps destroyed, and their fields burned. This was the last of the Indian hostilities until the first English settlement.

When the early pioneers settled the island in 1661, it was with the stated purpose of establishing a plantation like those in Providence Plantations. The first settlers were hard and rugged people. The islanders cleared the fields of surface rocks and trees, creating large pastures, which provided grazing for sheep and cattle.

Following trouble with the Indians, as well as raids from pirates and French privateers, the settlers selected a place at the highest and most visible point of the island, known as Beacon Hill. A large pile of wood was constructed, ready to ignite at a moment's notice. The bonfire would alert any islanders out at sea and friends on the mainland that the island was in need of rescue.

The island is noted for the increasing number of ships being lost upon her rocky shores. The following poem was penned by an Islander sailor who had been shipwrecked upon Block Island three times:

What Manner of Angel?

Three leagues of choppy sea from the mainland,
to this angelic cut of an emerald isle.
A mutton chop measured east to west,
and north to south just three by eight mile.
Her hills and hollows make the Irishman weep,
to think of home then fondly he will smile.
Thar she is, an angel's jewel, set in blue,
seemingly innocent and without guile.

Her pools of fresh water and a Great Salt pond,
teeming with fish frisky as they spawn
Can there possibly be any more breathtaking views,
then from island bluffs at dusk as well as dawn?

The hearty souls who settled this rugged oasis,
prosper for their bravery, brains and brawn
While timber and wildlife abound as with the natives,
how soon might they all be gone?

Her fresh tall green grasses waving
a welcome from the sandy dune.
To a glistening diamond stretch of beach,
shaped like a shiny crescent moon.
The cool summer breezes under dazzling starlight,
inspire the hum of a rich and dreamy tune.
And with the autumn twilight comes a sad thought,
of just how distant is the warmth of June.

But don't be mistaken by balmy summer breezes, mate,
don't dare be in denial.
Those angelic breezes will turn to winter blows,
filled with biting venomous bile.
Her rocky reefs claim ship by ship,
as their numbers continue to compile.
She looks soft and green but her soil breaks the plow,
to turn out rock and stone by the pile.

There's something cold, hard and jagged,
on the other side of an angel's summer bliss.
Both the shovel and the ship strike hard,
upon her bowlders few can scarcely miss.
From her soil the rock stretches out to sea
extending to the mariner her stony kiss.
Thrice the survivor cries out from the pebbly beach,
"What manner of angel is this?"

Giddy closed the book and returned it to the shelf. Some of the information would prove helpful, and he would make sure he took full advantage of it. He looked back down at the map, putting his finger on the small island.

Block Island? Block Island. Gilcox rubbed his dry, chapped chin as he strained to remember. *The name of this place is so damn familiar. I know this place, but how?*

"Yes, of course–it was Williams," he whispered out loud as his memory surfaced.

That second rate pirate Paulsgrave Williams hailed from this place called Block Island. Yes, he ended up a useless old man living in a pirate settlement in the Bahamas. Giddy pondered, *What was it? Something had scared Williams back in '17 to give up the pirate trade. He and his spineless mates took a pardon through the king's proclamation offered in the fall of that year and tried to make honest men of themselves. Fools.*

A painful knot formed in Giddy's stomach as he realized why he knew of Williams. Williams commanded the sloop *Mary Anne* and sailed as part of the fleet of Black Sam Bellamy when he captained the cursed *Whydah.*

Giddy felt sick and his knees grew strangely weak. He sensed an unfamiliar feeling of panic begin to come over him. He could not escape the haunting evil that continued to follow him from the Spanish slave ship.

"Damn my blood and damn her timbers!" Giddy barked.

Now he had second thoughts of using Block Island to deposit his treasure. Perhaps he should avoid this island altogether and find another location?

"No!" Giddy's anger exploded to overwhelm his fear. He grabbed and pulled the scraggly hairs on his cheeks with both fists and roared, "No!"

He would not allow himself to succumb to this irrational fear. He shook his head violently and forced himself to think clearly. *Williams survived the storm because he did not follow Black Sam to Cape Cod. That's right; he detoured to Block Island to visit his mum. That detour saved his life. It was Black Sam and the slave ship Whydah that were cursed!*

Giddy stopped and took several long, deep breaths to calm himself. He spoke out loud in a steady, reassuring tone, "Yes, it will be Block Island. That is our destination. This is the place to bury the treasure."

He looked back down at the map again. Pointing to the island on the map, he slid his finger north to the coast and followed the coast eastward. He spotted Cape Cod where Black Sam had met his fate. He shook his head once more, reminding himself that he didn't believe in spirits—he was the master, and he was in control. But the fear wouldn't completely let go, and he was becoming convinced that the evil from the Spanish slave ship had now visited upon his ship. It only made him more certain that he must complete his plan to find a replacement vessel and destroy the *Rogue Flattery*.

Chapter Twenty Two

In the bowels of the *Rogue Flattery*, Helen held her son tightly to her chest. The two huddled together, trying to bring each other comfort. The dark, rat-infested hold in which they were locked only heightened their fear. She was horribly seasick, and her son had already vomited several times.

Her sickness started with the heart-wrenching screams of a poor soul under torture by the pirates—that poor soul was, unmistakably, her husband. As she and William Jr. had been brought on board the pirates' ship, Helen saw a group of pirates, crowding in a circle. They were in a frenzy of punching, kicking, slapping, and stabbing at someone, and she knew it was William. For her son's sake, she swallowed her screams, just as she knew her husband took the beating quietly for their sake.

The anger she saw in these pirates horrified her. What had her family done to them to deserve such treatment? Was it that a colonial official represented the rules and authority they so disdained? Were they more than happy to get a measure of revenge for the merciless treatment they may have received in the past?

Finally, she knew that the punishment had become too much for her husband. His screams worked their way through the ship's hull to their ears. The boy held her more tightly and started sobbing. She wanted to tell him it was not his father he heard screaming, but instead, she broke down and sobbed with the boy.

On top of their emotional sickness came the nausea from the ship's incessant bouncing and twisting and turning. They were not seafaring people, and both vomited until they could no more. Even in her sickness, Helen recognized that the ship had to be moving exceedingly fast. When the ship seemed to slow, the repetitious, violent jolting shifted to a milder rocking and pitching, and she and William settled down a bit. Helen quietly sang hymns to little William, but he still stayed tight to her chest, clutching the gold cross.

As they became somewhat acclimated to their surroundings and the darkness, Helen began searching the hold. With the little light that seeped through the cracks in the hatchway, she found the room filled with sail, timber, hardware, and rope, as well as a few kegs of rum. She also found an iron bar that she briefly considered using as a weapon, but then thought that perhaps she might pry the door open, if the right opportunity presented itself. She hid the bar and then searched for something to use as a blanket to ward off their shivering.

Behind some of the rigging, she spied a piece of canvas. Helen reached through the rigging, grabbed hold, and pulled. As the canvas came loose, she saw a sight that caused her heart to jump into her throat and render her speechless.

Buried beneath all the tackle and rigging—and now exposed— was a man, tied to a chair, who appeared to have rotted away as he sat there. A rope was wound around his neck, and remnants of canvas covered his head. He had obviously been there a very long time and now sat as a skeleton, with some dried skin and hair still remaining. Not even the rats were interested any longer.

Several days had gone by without contact from the pirates. Helen wondered if the pirates had forgotten about their captives. In a sense, that brought some hope, but on the other hand, Helen feared they might end up like the poor creature in the chair. She and her son had both become very weak, but while William Jr. slept, she searched for anything that could help their situation. She did find a small porthole that had been boarded over. Perhaps she could break through it. It certainly was big enough for William to slip through, but she was not sure if she could fit.

As the time passed, Helen did her best to make a game of the situation with William and comforted him with prayers and uplifting hymns. He complained of hunger and thirst. She had just reached the point of demanding food and water from the pirates when she heard someone at the door, loosening the bolt.

A small, wiry pirate with a long nose entered. He held a plate of food and a cup of water. He looked down across his nose and made a face that suggested he had expected to find something different than the two of them huddled together, shivering.

"'Ungry?" he asked as he put the plate on the floor. "Enjoin' ya stay wid Mistah Gilcox?" He emitted a high-pitched cackle before backing out and bolting the door.

The two crawled to the plate. Helen was at first repulsed by the meal of moldy bread and a slimy gruel, but after a brief prayer, she and William devoured every morsel.

Some time later, two pirates entered the hold, and one said, "The cap'n wants you, mum. Leave da boy behind and come wid us."

"I cannot leave my boy," Helen insisted. "He must come with me." She reached for William, but they grabbed her, pushing William aside, and dragged her out. She could hear the door slam behind them, trapping her son inside.

Helen could hear William crying out for her. She tried her best to calmly call back, "Do not worry, William. I shall return shortly."

His weeping only grew louder at the sound of her voice. She prayed silently for strength enough to break free and run back to her son. All she wanted at that moment was to hold her son and allow him to feel the warmth of her comforting arms, hear the sound of her calming voice, and rest his head on her soft bosom while he played with her cross.

Helen tried to resist the pirates for a moment, but they tightened their grip and forced her to walk with them. Her heart sank. *Why is all of this happening?* she wondered. *Where is my God in all this?* She desperately wanted to believe she would return to her son, but she began to doubt that she would ever see young William again.

~~~

Giddy stood inside his cabin with his back to the door. He could hear the woman being dragged in and thrown down to the floor behind him. Without turning around, he raised his hand up and waved away the pirates. "Go. Leave us."

He heard the door close as the two pirates left, but he remained with his back to Helen. He wanted to see if her reaction to him was the same as the first time she had seen him. He took off his hat and wheeled around but found her kneeling, with her hands clasped and her eyes closed.

"Woman, look at me!"

Though she did not have the same reaction—she looked tired and weary—there was not one ounce of fear in her eyes as she looked up at him. He was used to the emotional displays of his captives who hysterically begged for mercy.

"Look at me, woman! What do you see?"

She shook her head and tenderly responded, "I see a poor, disfigured man, carrying a lifetime of pain and abuse."

The words hit like a sledgehammer between Giddy's eyes. The truth she spoke shook him to his core, and he turned away from her, covering his face with his hands. He could feel emotion welling up to the point that he thought he might actually burst into tears, but he refused to be touched in this way; he willed this emotion into anger.

He grabbed a heavy candlestick on the table next to him, intending to bash the side of her skull. When he wheeled back around, all he wanted to do was feel the crushing blow that would end her life.

The woman knelt there calmly, expecting and ready to receive the blow. As Giddy drew his arm back and began to bring it forward with full force, a glint from her gold cross caught his eye. It didn't cause him to flinch or even to blink, but at the very same moment, he felt a hand from behind grab his wrist, stopping his arm from delivering the blow.

He wheeled around with his arm cocked—but no one was there. Stunned, Giddy dropped the candlestick. His seething anger turned to bewilderment. He felt his wrist as he continued to look around his cabin. "Who is there?" he demanded. "Show yourself!"

There was no answer. Giddy turned back to the woman to see her in the same position, as if still waiting for the blow to come. He shook his head and called for the two pirates. When they entered, Giddy's voice was small and distant. "Take her away."

The men grabbed Helen, pulling her to her feet. Just as they reached the door, Gilcox commanded, "Stop!" He walked over to her, his eyes transfixed on her neck. He reached down, and for a moment she thought he intended to strangle her with one hand, but instead, he quickly snatched at the cross. With one yank, he broke the chain from around her neck.

Helen could no longer hold back her sobs, and her reaction made Giddy feel better. He looked at her and flashed an evil grin. Although she had escaped the blow from the candlestick, he now felt as though he had crushed the life out of her just the same. He turned and went back to his desk, and while staring at the cross in the one hand, he waved with his other hand to the pirates to take her away. "Be gone."

~~~

When the pirates threw Helen back in the hold, she immediately scrambled to hug her son, while silently thanking God for the chance to see him once again. William Jr. returned to his familiar position.

Though blinded by the light that came through the door as it was opened, they were now in almost total darkness again, and young William felt for the cross around his mother's neck. He groaned, "Mum, they've taken our Jesus."

Helen, choking back tears, replied, "No, I gave the cross to the captain so God could use it for a great thing. The one thing they can never take away is our Jesus." The words came without thought and brought as much comfort to her as they did to the boy.

Chapter Twenty Three

Within a few days, the *Rogue Flattery* had approached her destination. Gilcox was pleased with her progress, but the crew was becoming uneasy. He had already had to make examples of a few of the men. The buccaneers were itching to have at the supply of rum, and many were clamoring to get at the female hostage.

He knew that both rum and the woman could cause division and trouble on his ship. He denied them access to both, but trouble still brewed. Giddy was certain Niko, in particular, was looking amongst the crew to instigate mutiny, as Giddy was sure he had done on the Spanish galley. Giddy had to keep reminding himself that he needed the Greek so Niko eventually would unwittingly lead the others into the captain's plan.

It was early morning when they dropped anchor off the south end of Block Island. Giddy stood on deck, surveying the location. There were no ships in sight; the shoreline was rocky and rough with steep bluffs all along. Lush, green forest and vegetation covered the top of the bluffs.

"Mr. Blackbury!" he hollered. "Lower the longboat and transfer the treasure." He turned to the bosun. "Mr. Newsome, I'm leaving you in charge. I don't expect this will take long, so please keep a low profile until we return. We don't need any islanders discovering us and igniting their warning lantern to bring His Majesty's ships down upon us. See to it that the men stay sober and keep their filthy hands off the hostages. I promise there will be a taste of both in store for all when I return."

The longboat was loaded with Gilcox, First Mate Blackbury, Sachumjuia, and six other crew. A large chest was filled with the king's silver and gold, along with miscellaneous treasure picked up during their voyage north. Also on board were several muskets, water bags, and picks and shovels to complete their task. The boat sat low in the water.

As they rowed the boat closer to shore, Giddy saw that the beach was not made up of sand but piles of small stones and rock. The waves were very large, pounding the beach. Landing would be trickier than he had anticipated.

Giddy called out, "She must ride upon the shoulders of the largest of the three brothers, men! Steady! Steady! Not too fast, or we will be pitched over and buried in an instant!"

The men at the oars worked their way into the waves and waited as the waves rolled under them. Giddy looked forward and back and then shouted, "Now, soldiers! Pull with all your might!"

The men rowed furiously and soon the longboat was lifted high into the air under the largest "third brother". Giddy shouted, "Halt your rowing, men, and keep your balance!"

As the other men sat in breathless silence, Giddy stood and yelled in exhilaration over the din, "She rides! She rides!"

The longboat rode the large wave into shore, and two of the crew quickly jumped out on either side to guide the boat safely up onto the stony beach before the next wave could crash down upon them. The shore party pulled the boat up and, because of the terrible footing from the stones, awkwardly scrambled up to the bottom of the bluff. A natural cut in the bluff caused by rainwater erosion made a winding path up the dark brown clay of the bluff.

Giddy surveyed the terrain and realized that what he had read in his cabin days earlier concerning this island was proving to be true. "We'll take a moment to rest and then take this route up to the top."

In the clear dawn, Giddy sat on the treasure chest, staring out to his beloved ship. He continued to wrestle with himself over having to destroy so perfect a vessel, but he knew he must.

He looked off to the east at the large orange sun breaking over the horizon. The surf seemed louder than he ever remembered. Suddenly, what the woman had said about his lifelong suffering popped back into his mind. He'd played it in his head over and over, and each time, he had to keep denying its truth. To survive and cover the pain, he would convince himself that he was the great master and captain. People feared him, he told himself, for his great intellect, strength, and power. To believe otherwise would be to acknowledge that people's fear was due to that which he could not control—his physical features.

As Giddy pondered it all, he closed his eyes and heard a great applause. Over and over again, a tremendous throng of people were celebrating his greatness. The pirate captain stood up and lifted his arms with his hands facing up. He smiled and slowly turned, nodding his head repeatedly as he acknowledged the adoring crowd from one end of the beach to the other.

The pirates stared at one another, until one of them whispered, "Blimey, we's always known our cap'n's brilliant and a bit mad—one comes wid da other—but dis is a strange sight, aye!"

As Giddy acted this out, picturing himself addressing the crowd, all the crew could hear was the deafening sound of the waves crashing on shore. The water rushed up onto the stony beach, followed by the pull of the undertow dragging the water back into the sea, as the stones clapped against one another. Thousands and thousands of stones clapped together, creating the great applause that only Giddy could hear.

Abruptly, Giddy's mind snapped back to the shore party, and he ordered the group to proceed up the bluff; once there, Giddy led the way into the forest. He didn't plan to go very far into the forest to dig, but each time they broke earth, the roots and rock seemed impenetrable, so they moved farther in. Finally, they came to a small clearing, and he ordered, "Soldiers, this is the spot. This is where you will dig."

As they dug, the crew cursed, for with every swing of the pick and every dig of the shovel, they struck rock. The dig was taking much longer than Giddy had planned. "We'll sacrifice the usual depth," he conceded. "We'll be back for her shortly. This one can be shallower than usual."

One of the crew spoke up, looking around the dense forest. "Cap'n, how will we find da treasha when we return?"

Giddy glared at the pirate, meaning to quiet him. "Why *you* would need to know, soldier, is beyond even my intellect. But suffice it to say that I have already mapped it out in my mind. It will be a short time before our return, and I shall not be troubled in my recall. However, if your question has a tone of mistrust or concern that something will shortly happen to your captain, then I will mark the spot."

The shore party continued to struggle with rock as they dug the hole. Suddenly, they heard cannon fire in the distance.

"It must be a small boat that stumbled upon the ship," Giddy mused. "Let us hope that bugger Stroppy has disposed of it already. Continue your digging, you sorry sods."

Chapter Twenty Four

The young Manissean Indian boy quietly squatted on his haunches and observed. He mindlessly sifted his hands through the sandy soil while his eyes followed the two sinewy, glistening black arms that rose higher and higher into the air, growing darker in contrast with the clear blue sky. *Yes*, Quepag decided, *the wet black arms are much like the skin of the water snake.*

The muscular black arms stretched higher, raising the tool up and up and up, until they stopped at their highest point. They then hung suspended for a brief moment. Quepag smiled in anticipation of what would come next. The weight of the tool started the arc back down toward the earth. The hands and arms began pulling down, accelerating the tool to send it deep into the island soil.

When the iron point reached the ground, it came to a jolting stop with a loud clink. The stone it hit would not give way, and the shock vibration ran back up the axe handle and into the black arms, shaking the entire body of the slave. Quepag winced and felt his own body quiver at the jarring impact.

The second slave, working the shovel, was not making much progress either. The small amount of dirt loosened by the pick axe was scraped across the jagged stone. The sound made Quepag involuntarily clench his teeth and caused his hair to stand on end.

The sounds of the slaves at work rolled down into the lush green of the hollow and up the other side to echo back to them. The progress on the dig was moving slowly, and the young boy was growing restless.

Quepag's ears pricked up and his brow furrowed as he noticed something strange in the echo. Many in his tribe often called him "Animosh", after the island's wild dogs, because of his keen sense of hearing. Now he noticed that the echo was not the same as the first sound. He was angry with the white man and with the slaves, so he hadn't intended to speak one word to anyone while indentured, but his curiosity caused him to announce, "There are others digging."

The elder slave, Titus, ignored the boy at first, but amidst the sounds of the digging, he asked, "What was dat ya say, Indian? Ya been quiet for days. Now what ya have ta say?"

The two young slaves digging in the hole paused, looking for any excuse to stop their painful enterprise.

Putting his hand up, Quepag signaled the others to be quiet. "Hear the digging?"

The black men looked at each other, shook their heads, and went back to work. Titus spoke in an agitated tone. "Boy, ya hearin' us dig, and de echoes is comin' back ta us. Now ya just stay hushed up."

Quepag shook his head in disgust that these grown men could not hear what he heard.

Titus turned to the two young slaves in the hole and said, "Ya two climb on out of dat hole. Stepney and Cuff, gets in der and show dem new boys how ta pull out dat confounded island rock."

The two young slaves had only been on Block Island for a few months and were not familiar with the particular challenges of excavating the almost impenetrable rock-and-stone soil. Stepney and Cuff were older and more experienced with the island. During their time on the island, they had excavated tons of rock and built miles of stone walls.

They each picked up long iron rods with ends that had been hammered to a flat edge and stepped down into the shallow hole, confident of making headway. Locating the gaps between the rocks, they lifted the bars over their heads, thrust the flat edge into the soil between the rocks, and then worked the bars back and forth to loosen up the rock and dirt. After some time at this, the two climbed back out and the younger two jumped back in to remove what had been loosened.

Quepag was distracted as he listened for the other sounds. He looked back at the slaves' work in frustration. The process would continue until the tops of their heads were just below the ground surface. At this pace, how long would it take? The boy shook his head. It would take a long time.

Large Titus was supervising as Quepag worked out a sentence of servitude—he'd been caught stealing one of the Hawkins' pigs. Wherever Titus went, Quepag had to go, too.

The slaves' master—the white man, Hawkins—had chosen this place to dig. After two days of Master Hawkins' keeping himself behind the closed doors of the library, the house mum, Molly, had convinced her master to finally bury the woman they all called Miz Elizabet. The white man's wife lay cold in her casket. The birth of their baby child had turned happy excitement to sorrow—his woman had not awakened after the birth, and now they were saying that the baby was sickly, too.

Master Hawkins had become so crazy with anguish and grief that it didn't seem he would have the strength to make a decision. But finally, he called for his senior slave, Titus, and described where he wanted his wife buried. He wanted her to rest on the southeast corner of the plantation, at the highest point, just below the crest of the island hollow. With a crazed look in his eyes, he said, "From there, I can join my precious treasure so that we both may look back over the rolling ravine to our lovely plantation house and hear the sound of the majestic surf on the beach from the other side of the crest."

Quepag looked over the work party that was made up of five of Hawkins's adult male slaves: the large, dark Titus; the mulatto, Cuff; and the brown-skinned Stepney; and two new acquisitions, dark Africans named Bolico and Cujo.

The eight-year-old Indian boy had been part of the slaves' work parties before. When the slaves were off on their own, they usually would be playful, but this time, a sadness hung over the group. Quepag didn't really know the woman, Miz Elizabet, but they all seemed to have deep feelings for her. Quepag heard them say that she had been a very kind woman who had helped to soften the hardness of their master.

The new slaves, Bolico and Cujo, looked confused and scared.

Their homeland must still be fresh in their minds, Quepag thought. *Now they are thinking this is their home. Will the white woman's death mean everything will change again for them? Will they now be sent away to another place?*

They did not speak much English yet, but Quepag had heard Titus tell stories of what it was like to be dragged off from his homeland to this new and strange place. Quepag did not ever want to leave Manisses, even though the white men had come and changed much of their lives.

He observed all that had happened and was confused. All the emotions the family and their slaves were showing troubled him. To his people, death was another life. The Manissean people had another world waiting for them on the other side of this life. Both his mother and father died from one of the strange sicknesses the white men brought with them. Quepag had seen many of his people die, and still his tribe did not behave the way these slaves were behaving.

While he pondered the white woman's death, Quepag lost interest in the slave's work. He suddenly realized that the work party had dug down several feet into the hole. He turned his attention to the dig once again and watched the slave named Stepney thrust the point of the bar down. Just as it struck the ground, Quepag was surprised to hear a loud concussion. The other slaves were startled, too, and all looked down into the hole. They looked at each other, unsure of what they had just heard. Had the sound been caused by iron striking rock?

Quepag spoke first, for he knew what he had heard. "A cannon fired on the water, over past the other digging."

Chapter Twenty Five

Stroppy Newsome was relishing his time as captain of the *Rogue Flattery* while Gilcox was off burying the treasure. He was a bit anxious, unsure of what he would do if they were discovered. The rest of the buccaneers were milling around in a mixed state of boredom, impatience, and irritation: bored, for while anchored, there wasn't much to do except carry out Stroppy's contrived orders; impatient because of the kegs of rum and the female on board, neither of which they had touched in weeks; irritated because with the captain and Blackbury gone, Cortlaroy felt no restraint in getting his jollies by annoying all on board.

Stroppy knew Cortlaroy was growing more and more anxious to end his days at sea, now that the shores and cities of Europe seemed that much closer. He was clearly feeling freer to agitate the crew.

The old Irishman, Kinehan, was politicking Stroppy to break out some rum. "We're dyin', lad. We're buccaneers—'tis da trink dat keeps us alive! A mere jigger will brighten ar day an' improve ar dark shpirit."

Stroppy had to agree that he was concerned about the mood of the crew. Not only was the irritating quartermaster Cortlaroy causing trouble amongst the crew, but he didn't like the little Greek who was trying to incite the men. Stroppy didn't understand why Gilcox hadn't keelhauled him already.

Still, he wasn't going to have any part of breaking out the rum. Even though he was the senior officer left in charge, he didn't have the keys to the hold with the extra munitions and rum. Like most of the men, he was aware that some rum had been stored with Mr. Gilcox and the captives, but he knew Giddy would keelhaul him if the captain returned to a drunken crew.

Stroppy watched the Greek move from group to group of the pirates. It was a safe bet that he was using the rum and the woman as an opportunity to win the hearts of the men for mutiny. Whenever Stroppy saw him gather a group together, he would move to break them up.

The bosun knew that he was well hated by the men, but he also knew that they despised Chauncy Cortlaroy more and more, as he tried to provoke each man on board into a sword fight. This, along with the fact that the crew was deathly afraid of their captain, gave Stroppy security that the men would not revolt.

While the sun was at its highest, all was quiet and still. The crew milled about in a state of silent irritation. The only sounds were with the creaking of the ship and the flap of loose sail. Suddenly, an excited call came from one of the buccaneers. "Sail off starboard bow!"

A small sailboat had sailed around the point and now was not three hundred yards from the ship. Stroppy had already decided what to do under these circumstances—he would draw her in and sink her, making certain that all on board were eliminated.

Stroppy gave hushed orders. "Prepare da small swivel cannon on deck for firin'. The rest of ya salty sods, appears like ya goin' 'bout ya business."

The bosun pulled out a distress flag and ran it aloft to signal the small sailboat. The sailboat had two islander fishermen on board, and they appeared to be cautiously approaching to communicate with the crew.

The crew gathered to the cap rail and were humored by the quirky design of the little sailboat. One of the crew shouted back to the bosun, "Stroppy, ya ever seen a funny boat like 'at before?"

Stroppy was a student of shipbuilding and was knowledgeable of almost any craft afloat. He became very animated with his exuberance to show off his intelligence on the subject. "She's known as a *pinnace* but often referred ta as a *double-ender*, or as da fishermen calls 'em, *cow horns*. She has a keel at an angle of forty-five degrees which rises up da stern and stem posts, wid lapstreak sides, bows, and sterns nearly alike. She's open, wid two masts and narrow, tapering sails. One ta four tons burthen, sittin' deep in da water.

"A steady and safe little dorrie she is. Da ones I seen of carry beach stones used fa ballast set in da stern. What fishermen does is gather in da fish, and da weight of da fish replaces da stone ballast, and dey just throw dem stones overboard."

Stroppy paused for a moment to admire the island boat and then continued. "Boys, dis here boat may look peculiar, but she's seaworthy enough and can carry sail inta a strong headwind. She is a bloody pretty little thing. 'Tis a shame we're goin' ta make a mess of her."

As the double-ender sailed closer, the Greek approached Stroppy and challenged him in front of the crew. "I bet you one shot I can sink that small boat! Rum for all if I can do!"

Concerned about scaring off the sailboat, Stroppy resisted the urge to smack the Greek's head with the side of his cutlass.

Cortlaroy took the opportunity to needle Stroppy. "Well, well, Stroppy, you are an Englishman. Are you going to ignore the challenge from this less-than-human hairy creature? I thought you were at least as strong as that foul odor you emit."

The other men gathered around the two and began challenging Stroppy to take the Greek on.

"Aw right, den," Stroppy replied. "Ya git one shot, an' if ya hit her, it's rum aw round. If ya miss but I sink her, da rum is on me, and you git keehauwed!"

The Greek readily accepted the challenge and went directly to the gun. He waited as Stroppy yelled to the fishermen, "Ahoy, mates, we've got some ill men on board, and we anchored ta get fresh water. Can ya help us wid our sick sailors?"

Their craft drifted closer. As the fishermen strained to hear what Stroppy was saying, Niko aimed and lit the fuse. The fishermen saw the flame of the lit fuse and scrambled to get wind in their sail, but the gun fired. The ball went sailing right through their mainsail and snapped the mast.

Stroppy jeered, "A-ha, you hairy little devil."

Cortlaroy squealed with delight. "Now for some real entertainment!"

The Greek had failed, and Stroppy strode righteously over, pushed the Greek down, and reloaded for a second shot. The fishermen were struggling to get their remaining sail to catch wind but realized it was hopeless. Their only defense, then, was to pick up the stones used as ballast and hurl them at the pirates.

The first stone hit the ship with a smack, and the pirates roared with laughter at the futility of the fishermen's defense. Then one of the pirates dropped cold to the deck as a stone hit him square in the temple. Another stone hit a pirate in the chest and another in the mouth.

Stroppy was amazed at the accuracy of the fishermen. He yelled, "I'd take cover, men. Dese two seems 'at dey could hit seagulls right out of da sky!"

The pirates' laughter turned to cursing, and Stroppy hurried to get the ship's gun reloaded and his sight set. He fired and blasted the double-ender at the waterline. She sank within seconds. Stroppy lifted his hands in exultation and crowed, "Now that, my dirty scoundrels, is gunnery."

The blast left one of the fishermen floating face down in the water and the other trying to swim around the ship toward shore. Stroppy waved to two men to go in after them and finish the job.

The two pirates dove in with their knives sheathed to their side. They surfaced, and one swam to the unconscious fisherman and thrust a knife in his back several times. The other pirate quickly caught up with the second fisherman, and after a brief struggle, the fisherman floated away, motionlessly in blood-stained water.

All the buccaneers cheered at their exhilarating sport—all except for one.

Stroppy smiled at the Greek. He saw Niko's anger boiling up as he leaned against the rail and stared back at the bosun. Not only had he missed the shot, but Stroppy had enjoyed further embarrassing him by pushing him down.

Stroppy taunted him, "I'm goin' ta recommend ta da cap'n for you ta be keehauwed for bein' a miserable shot and for all your trouble-makin'!"

Niko looked at Stroppy with murderous eyes.

Stroppy knew what he was thinking and said imperiously, "Ya think ya can take me, ya just try. Ya're not strong enough to hurt old Stroppy. I'll squash ya like da little maggot ya're."

Chauncy was delighted with the exchange. He called out, "Brilliant! We shall see what we can do to make this most entertaining!"

Stroppy was enthralled with his personal victory. Now, feeling like the captain, he ordered, "Rum for everyone, ya scurvy scoundrels—everyone except the Greek!"

The men cheered, but Stroppy knew that there were more than a few pirates who would not side with him if there were a fight. Many had suffered under his heavy hand at one time or another.

"You three," Stroppy ordered to the nearest crewmen, "go down below ta Mr. Gilcox's quarters and retrieve da hidden rum from da hold. Don't ya dare lay a hand on da hostages, or I'll cut it off, ya hear me?"

Chapter Twenty Six

Helen had lost almost all perspective of time, but it seemed that a day or more had passed when a commotion arose on deck, and she heard the splash of the anchor. She told William to remain quiet as she listened and tried to make sense of what she was hearing.

A mixture of hope and fear began to rise up in Helen. This might mean a change in their circumstances, although whether good or bad, she did not know. As she listened, she heard something banging down the side of the ship, and then heard what sounded like scurrying down the side. Helen concluded that a boat had been lowered and that some of the pirates were leaving the ship.

Hours seemed to pass before she finally heard activity on deck, followed by a blast from a cannon. At first, the pirates shouted and cursed, but that was followed by the sound of objects pelting the ship. The pirates' cursing turned to laughter, but then the laughter suddenly ceased, followed a moment later by the sound of another blast from the cannon and a loud cheer from the pirates. Helen concluded that the pirates were engaging in target practice.

Shortly after the commotion, a group of pirates abruptly came through the door. They stood there, looking at the two hostages for a moment. The dirty, lustful looks scared her almost as much as Giddy's hideous features. Two of them stayed at the door, but one came tiptoeing in, keeping his distance from them, as if they might pounce on him.

The pirate spoke up. "You are a might fortunate—da cap'n said hands off. We'd be 'avin' some fun wid ya. Giddy thought 'e'd locked up all da rum, but we hid some here wid his fadder."

He handed a keg to each man and then took one himself. As he was leaving, he said, "I trust ol' Mistah Gilcox 'as been a po-lite 'ost. He's not much fa conversation, but he's a good lisna!" The three laughed as they closed and bolted the door.

Helen knew that all the pirate talk was beyond her son's comprehension, but it left her wondering if their reference to Gilcox's father could possibly be true. *Is that really the remains of the captain's father?* She could not believe any human being was capable of such a horrible thing.

More hours passed, and the ship continued to steadily rock on anchor. Helen tried to listen through the hull and could faintly hear surf pounding on a beach, followed by a noise like applause at a large concert hall. The sound was repeated over and over. Occasionally, she could hear seagulls squawking as they circled around the ship. She was tempted to take the bar and try to pry open the porthole— they were near land and might have a chance to escape. She realized, though, that it would take a strong swimmer to get through the waves, and she didn't know if either of them would make it.

Finally, Helen decided to try to loosen the boards. To her surprise, she found they loosened quite easily, and light started streaming into the dark hold.

This raised her spirits. The light illuminated William's face, and he smiled at her, which raised her spirits even more. Helen took a quick look out and then immediately covered the hole. All she had seen was a glimpse of the blue sky and ocean. The sound of the surf was on the other side of the ship, leaving the porthole facing out to sea.

Helen decided that she would wait until dark, finish opening the hole, and then see if they could both get through it to escape.

Chapter Twenty Seven

Topside on the *Rogue Flattery*, Stroppy felt good about himself. He had been victorious over the Greek and felt he had proven himself as a leader of the men. Now the pirates were enjoying their spirits, singing crude sailor songs, and telling boastful stories. The men drank hard, behaving as if they might never have another drink again.

Chauncy Cortlaroy strolled up to Stroppy and asked, "Mr. Newsome, are you aware of the dirty stares coming from our Greek friend?"

"I see his hairy face," the bosun replied. "He ain't no more than dirty looks. What's it matter to ya, Cortlaroy?"

"I've got some brilliant quips that will gloriously dress down that dirty Greek. He deserves a good verbal slap, and I'd be happy to provide you with some choice ammunition."

Stroppy grinned. "Aw right, I'll have at 'im. Let's roast da little pig."

After Chauncy whispered into the bosun's ear, Stroppy called out to Niko. "Hey, ya dirty four-footed animal. Ya're as short as a pig and twice as smelly."

The pirates gathered for the entertainment. One of the men in the crowd called out, "Sounds like ya describing ya'self, Stroppy!"

The pirates roared with laughter. Stroppy glared at Chauncy, but Chauncy ignored Stroppy's anger and came right back to whisper more insults for Stroppy to deliver to Niko.

"Dey says da Greeks is da cradle of civilization," Stroppy repeated out loud. "And I says dat it looks like da cradle is where ya belongs, ya pint-sized twit."

The men laughed and looked at Niko for his reaction.

Niko looked puzzled. "What is that you saying to me?"

"No, ya wouldn't understand because, by da looks of ya, ya mum was a black wooly sheep and ya fadda was a jackass."

The men laughed, and Niko answered, "You don't talk of my mama and baba like this!"

But Stroppy continued. "Oh, yeah? The Greeks—ain't dey da people where da men wear dresses and da women grows beards?"

Niko yelled back over the men's laughter. "You don't talk of my mama and baba like this!"

"Mama and baba?" Stroppy mimicked. "Real pirates don't talk like dat! Ya're no pirate; ya're just a wooly Greek fisherman, and ya'd be floatin' face down wid da other two fishermen we just kilt if I had any say in da matter!"

The Greek's anger was at its boiling point, but he did not respond. He was the only one not drinking, and he was restraining himself until the bosun was sufficiently drunk.

Stroppy understood Niko's plan, but he was confident that he could defeat Niko, even in a drunken state.

Some time later, Chauncy slid over to the Greek and whispered into his ear, "If ever there was a time to make your move, it would be now!"

With that, Niko strolled over to Stroppy, and they glared at each other.

"I have men with me to mutiny," Niko said, "so now you will die."

Stroppy chuckled as he took the words with mild amusement and disinterest.

The buccaneers looked around at each other, seemingly confused by Niko's suggestion that some were willing to mutiny. Stroppy saw the men's reactions and knew the Greek's move was premature. Stroppy was still confident that none was prepared to follow the Greek against Giddy. The pirates drunkenly looked about to consider who was friend and who was foe.

Stroppy stood up, suddenly realizing just how drunk he was as he staggered a bit. He was prepared, though, to end it quickly by drawing his flintlock and firing one shot. As he glanced nonchalantly to his side while reaching within his coat, he felt a punch to his chest and a burning pain. He looked down to find the handle of a knife sticking out of his chest. As fast as it registered in his mind what had happened, he saw the blade of a cutlass pass under his chin, and he felt the blade slice through his neck.

He underestimated the Greek's quickness. He barely moved before the Greek had thrown his knife. Stroppy grabbed his neck with his free hand. He started choking as blood poured from his chest and spouted from his neck. All this happened as he was still pulling the pistol from beneath his coat. Niko took another swing with his cutlass, but Stroppy, his pistol now free, pulled the trigger and shot the Greek in the face. Both dropped into a heap on the deck.

In a fit of gleeful exuberance, Cortlaroy pulled his sword to duel with anyone who would draw his. "Hee hee, now we shall have some real entertainment. Step right up, one by one, and take your chances, you foul-smelling seadogs!"

The rest of the drunken pirates all pulled their swords and started squaring off. All it took was for Chauncy to take one dramatic thrust to ignite the bloodbath. The pirates were so drunk that they didn't know which side they were on, but the instinct of self-preservation took over, and men slashed, stabbed, and cut each other without knowing who they struck or why.

A half-dozen pirates focused their anger and rage on the frilly little quartermaster, Cortlaroy. They converged on him, and although he killed several and wounded the others, he was eventually overwhelmed and was stabbed and beaten to death. The other pirates continued to drop left and right, and the few left alive collapsed from their wounds, exhausted and dying.

In no more than a quarter-hour's time, the ship's crew was decimated. The ship started rocking as the wind picked up and the sky darkened. The few who were still alive realized they were in for a blow, and their sailor instincts took over as they tried to muster the strength to prepare the ship. Soon, though, every man on board lay still and bleeding on the deck of the *Rogue Flattery*.

~~~

"Injun, now, ya be quiet," Titus snapped. "There ain't no diggin' other dan right here, and I don't know what or where dat sound come from. What I does know is dat de master be here soon wid Miz Elizabet, and we got ta finish dis hole and clean up ta be respectful. Now let's be finished."

Quepag was concerned. *Could a war party be attacking the island?* He was astonished that the sound had been of no interest to the slaves.

Once again, Stepney thrust his bar down and hit rock, just as another concussion boomed. Stepney dropped his bar and stood frozen as they all looked down at him.

Quepag's concern turned to fear. He could not keep himself silent. "It is small cannon on the water. We should go see." He got up and headed toward the ocean.

"Ya sit ya'self right down der, boy!" Titus barked. "Ya go off, and we'll never see ya's fa two weeks. Ya done stole dat pig, and de island fathers say ya's a slave ta Hawkins fa a month."

Disappointed, Quepag sat down.

"Keep movin', Negroes," Titus ordered the other men. "We gots ta hurry up and finish." Turning back to the Indian boy, he continued, "I don't knows how dis be punishment. Ya comes here, we feeds ya, and de master don't say to give you no work. It be just like lookin' after a baby."

With that comment, Quepag became angry. *Quepag not a baby!* He lived with his grandfather, the Sachem, who had taught him how to hunt and fish as well as any of the other island braves. As for the pig he had been accused of stealing, he knew that a large pig from his own tribe had sired it. Walking home past the Hawkins plantation, he'd found the pig on the trail. When he threw it some corn, the pig followed him home. Once Quepag had the pig home, he thought he had the right to keep him.

Quepag was so angry with Titus that he reached down and grabbed a rock to throw at him. Before he could toss it, he heard the shot. They all heard the shot. It wasn't as loud as the previous two, but the men had all paused in their work, so it was quiet when this shot echoed over the water.

They all turned to Titus to gauge his reaction. Titus now seemed more concerned by this new noise, but he tried to conceal it.

"Flintlock from on the water," Quepag anxiously reported.

Titus gave him an angry stare. "Must be someone huntin' on de shore. Now come, boys. What's I got ta do ta get ya's ta finish dis hole? Dey all waitin' fa us."

Quepag didn't believe it was a hunter, and he didn't think Titus believed it, either. The whole island was mourning and coming to the white woman's funeral.

Titus seemed nervous. He reassured the others. "If I hears one more shot, I's goin' ta look myself."

The men continued their dig. The work slowed down as they came across large boulders that were difficult to remove. Quepag was beside himself with frustration. Why didn't these men care to see who was making these sounds? He had heard of men who had come in the past to plunder the island, killing and wounding many men.

Suddenly, Quepag jumped up again. "Stop! Can't ya hear it?" he cried. "Men fighting! If you will not go, I will go see." He turned and ran off.

"Stop him!" Titus yelled to Cuff, who was sitting on a rock behind the boy.

Cuff dove, tackling Quepag by the ankles, and dragged him back to Titus. Quepag kicked his feet and struggled to get away, but Cuff was too strong. Titus took some rope from around his waist and used it to tie the boy's feet tightly together. "Now ya stay. By God, we gots to finish, and we can't be chasin' ya all over dis island." Turning to the others, he yelled, "Finish dis hole!"

Quepag was angry, and he thought, *These black men are stupid, or they have corn in their ears for not being able to hear what I can plainly hear.* Except for the fact that his feet were now tied, he wished that whatever war party was on the other side of the ridge would come over and make them pay for their stupidity.

~~~

When Giddy heard the second cannon shot, he cursed, roaring, "Bloody hell! Why don't we just invite the whole bloody island to tea? Blackbury, return to the bluff to see what's what and report back to me."

His first mate ran through the brush and returned minutes later, saying, "Dere was no other ships I saw, Cap'n. Nothin' unusual down dere, 'cept a few of da men swimmin' around da ship. I did see a storm brewing, movin' in from da sou'west."

"Soldiers," said Giddy uneasily, "we've got to finish this up and return to the ship. I have a bad feeling about this."

When the shore party finally put the treasure in the hole, only a foot of dirt covered their booty. As they finished filling in the hole, Giddy spoke up. "Hold your work, soldiers." He searched through his pockets and pulled out the gold cross and chain, saying, "Ah, this will do!" He then attached one end of the chain to an iron loop on the top of the chest. As they proceeded to fill the last of the soil over the treasure, he held out the cross as a marker. Giddy laid the cross on the dirt and said, "X marks the spot, soldiers! Roll a boulder here, and let us return to the ship." Giddy knew this would not provide much help in locating the treasure, but the gesture would satisfy the pirates' simple minds that he was not trying to take advantage.

In the time since Giddy had taken the cross from the woman, he had studied it to see if there was anything mystical or magical about it. He had a gnawing feeling that the cross had something to do with saving the woman's life, just when he had intended to kill her.

Since then, each time he held the cross, he had been visited by cold sweats and eerie sensations that he believed had come over from the Spanish slave ship. He was now convinced it held no power to ward off spirits, yet it seemed that it was somehow more than just a bit of gold and might actually cause evil to be visited upon him.

With the hole filled and the gold cross laid as a marker, the men struggled to roll a large boulder over the cross. They had just put the rock in place when they heard the flintlock shot.

Giddy wasn't sure if it had come from the ship or from someone on the island. The Mohegan Indian had disappeared to scout around as soon as the group climbed to the top of the bluff; he had not reappeared since. Giddy was feeling more unsettled. The sky was now very dark, and the wind was beginning to blow, bending branches and whipping leaves about.

Giddy called out in the growing wind, "Men, back to the *Rogue Flattery* with haste!"

When they made it back to the top of the bluff, Giddy's sense of alarm increased. A tremendous storm was closing in fast. The wind was howling, and the sea was already growing rough. The rain started to fall hard, with lightning and thunder in the distance. Sachumjuia was nowhere in sight, but Giddy could not wait for him. What they saw when they looked toward their ship made the whole party run down the path to the beach. The *Rogue Flattery* was being pushed dangerously close to shore.

From Giddy's vantage on the bluff he could see virtually no activity on the ship. Nothing had been done to batten down the ship for the storm or to prepare her to be moved farther out to sea. The shore offered no protection from the storm, and the *Rogue Flattery* would soon be on the rocks if they could not get her underway. The group scrambled to the longboat and carried it down to the water's edge. The waves had grown even larger in size, and it took them several tries to get through the first series of breakers.

Gilcox was not a man accustomed to fear, but when they approached the ship and no one looked over the rail to greet them, he smelled disaster. As the longboat pulled alongside, the men, led by their captain, climbed up the side of the ship. The last man out, panicking, let the longboat wash away. As Giddy came over the railing, he was completely and utterly dumbfounded. He could not fathom what might have taken place, but the sight of every man on board lying in a pool of blood left his mind racing with possibilities. Giddy wanted answers, but there was no time to waste on asking questions.

With just eight pirates, they would have to find a way to quickly move the *Rogue Flattery* farther out to sea. Giddy manned the helm and gave orders. "Blackbury, be at the ready with a hatchet to the anchor line! All you others, move quickly to let out some sail from the main mast. See that the sail is as taut as possible. Don't let it be torn or let it fly loosely by the wind."

Giddy knew that this was a dangerous undertaking and to be handled successfully, it would typically require many more hands. He also knew he had only one chance. Still, when it came to sailing, he was the most confident man alive.

Using the anchor as a lever, they would drop the main sail to catch the full draft of the wind from the southwest. He would pull the wheel hard to the starboard, and if the sail, mast, and rigging could hold against the gale, the *Rogue Flattery* would swing around by the anchor line, out to the open sea. Giddy would then signal his first mate to cut the anchor line, the crew would trim the sails, and they would move away from shore before hunkering down to ride out the storm.

It all worked perfectly; Blackbury chopped the anchor line and they headed out to sea, but for every length of forward gain, they were pushed three lengths to port by the weather. Still, Gilcox was certain they had missed the rocks, and despite the chaos that had visited his ship, he basked in the exhilaration of his own brilliance.

Chapter Twenty Eight

Helen wondered if now was the time to make their escape. Perhaps she could find something small enough to fit through the opening that would float to help them get to shore. She found a good-sized piece of cork that was fashioned into a buoy, with a rope loop coming out of the end. She instructed William that once he was out, he should hold tight to the buoy to help him float.

Helen could hear the pirates on deck—their voices grew louder, and their language became harsher and more violent. Then she heard what she thought was a pistol shot.

The loud, brash sailor songs suddenly changed to cursing, yelling, and fighting. The sounds of metal striking metal grew louder, telling Helen that this might cause a change in their situation, although she was uncertain if this would be good or very bad. The possibility remained that whoever prevailed might disregard the captain's orders and come down to take advantage of them.

Helen's fear persuaded her that the time might be right, while the pirates were occupied, to make their escape. She pried a board up to check the light and was surprised at how quickly it had turned dark. Her instincts told her now was the time to act.

She started frantically prying off the remaining boards. It became more difficult to steady herself as the ship started to pitch violently. The saltwater sprayed in her face, and the howl of the wind awoke her to the fact that a major storm was arriving. She was now reluctant to go ahead with her plan, convinced that neither of them could survive in a rough sea.

The din on the top deck grew silent, but soon there came a familiar banging on the side of the ship. Helen thought that the shore party must have returned. She could hear voices again and orders being barked out. Within minutes, the ship surged forward and listed heavily to the port side. Helen and William rolled across the hold. The ship again was under sail and was now bouncing through what had become very choppy seas.

Helen heard more shouting and screaming, and then a terrible crash. The ship stopped dead in the water. Helen and William, along with everything in the hold, were thrown forward toward the bulkhead. The ship was shuddering and shaking, and the floor in front of them began dropping down.

Helen was shaken and confused, and William was crying. As Helen struggled to get her bearings, she heard more screaming and yelling from the pirates. Amongst all the noise, wind, and unintelligible yelling, Helen heard only one word clearly: "Abandon." She realized that there would be no other opportunity for escape. The ship pitched forward, and water started coming in under the door—the decision had been made for her. Helen quickly told William what had to be done as she pried the boards, caulking, and rusted metal from the hull. They now had to stand partially on one of the ship ribs in order to stay erect.

Helen considered going first, but she was not certain she would fit through the hole. With the opening clear, Helen immediately grabbed the buoy that, by fortune, had floated up next to them in the rising waters. She then picked up William to push him through the hole. She could see the water outside just a few feet below.

William resisted and cried out, "No, Mum, I won't go!"

Helen shook him and said, "You must! And you must hold onto this buoy with all your might!"

William was stunned—his mother had never before spoken to him in this way. He responded immediately to her instruction. He went through the hole, feet first, and disappeared into the turbulent waters. Helen anxiously watched for what seemed a lifetime until, to her relief, William bounced up, holding the buoy.

Helen now struggled to get through the hole. She was able to push her head, shoulders, and right arm through, but her left arm became pinned to her body. Helen strained to push through, but she was hopelessly stuck at her waist.

The water rose up over the hole, and Helen tried desperately to free herself, even as she, along with the entire ship and its crew, were swiftly slipping below the surface of the water. She caught one last glimpse of William and raised her hand, not to wave good-bye but more to say, *I'm over here! I'll always be here!*

Once below the surface, Helen continued to struggle. After a minute, a warm calm came over her. Everything suddenly seemed to speak to her so clearly. She knew that all this pain, anguish, and fear soon would be behind her. She now looked forward to residing in a world without terrible inhumanities as she rested serenely with her Savior.

Helen heard someone behind her calling in a familiar way. Without thinking, she responded, "William, I do tell, for your lass and your boy, all is well!" Her eyes closed, and she felt a warmth on her face as she blushed.

~~~

When young William went into the water, he immediately felt the shock of icy needles poking him all over. The water was so cold, and he couldn't help taking a big swallow of the salty sea. He coughed up the briny drink as he surfaced, but he had lost the buoy! He grabbed and kicked to get it back, but he couldn't see anything. Without understanding how, the rope loop had wrapped completely around his chest and under his arms. It was tight and painful, with the buoy hitting him in the nose when he surfaced and bounced in the waves. He grabbed it and held it tight and pressed his face against it.

The boy struggled in the heavy waves, and when he opened his eyes again, they stung from the salt. As one wave crested, lifting him up, he caught a glimpse of his mother coming out of the porthole. He slipped in a trough between the waves, and when he rose up again, his mother's hand was slipping below the surface. The whole ship quickly followed, and as the last part of the deck went under the sea, William saw the pirate captain. The hideous man was entangled in collapsed rigging and pumping his fist, shouting heavenward, before he was dragged under with the rest of the ship.

William gasped, and the world seemed to grow quiet. Suddenly, a great pull sucked him and everything floating around him right down. He didn't even get a chance to take a breath before everything went black.

Chapter Twenty Nine

Stepney climbed down into the hole—it was now too tight and too deep for more than one man. They had begun taking turns, climbing in to remove the last foot of earth and rock. Now Stepney would finish the job. He felt a sense of honor, knowing he would be the last to go in before Miss Elizabeth. Stepney slipped and fell onto his back, landing with a thud that knocked the wind from him. The cold, moist rock and soil beneath him made him shiver. Looking up from the bottom of the grave, it appeared as if the opening was a mile away, and he pictured the earthen walls caving in on top of him. The thought of being buried there flashed in his mind, gripping him with fear. He sprang to his feet and tried to shake off the dirt and cold. His heart raced.

Leaning back against the grave wall, he began to cry. He tried as hard as he could to control himself and to keep the others from seeing him, but the harder he tried, the more the sobs wanted to come out. His body began to convulse from the struggle.

Cujo and Bolico were standing near the edge of the hole and looked in to see if Stepney was hurt. When they saw him shaking, they were confused. Cujo spoke to Titus in his limited English, "Stepney, hurt?"

Titus looked in the hole and climbed down. Once in the hole, he grabbed Stepney's shoulders and asked, "What's happened? Is ya hurt?"

Tears streamed down Stepney's face. Titus waved away the two staring from above. "Ya boys go sit down wid Cuff and leave us be."

"What's wrong wid ya?" Titus asked. "What's happened, Stepney? Is ya hurt? Why ya be cryin'?"

Stepney tried to straighten himself up and wipe away the tears, but his sobbing would not stop. The floodgates were open, and there was little he could do. Between sobs, he blurted out, "I just founds out my Molly is wid child, and here she is all broke up over Miz Elizabeth. I don't wants dem ta die, too." He leaned forward and put his head on the bigger man's shoulder. "Why does God has ta always take de good ones? Why do dey has ta die?" Stepney felt that the world as he knew it was surely coming apart. Only a few short days earlier, the family had been excited about the imminent arrival of the Hawkins' first child. Master Hawkins was in his finest mood. Adding to the joy, the house mum, Molly, had informed Stepney that she was carrying his child. Now, so suddenly, Miss Elizabeth was gone, her child was struggling to survive, his Molly was sick and inconsolable, and Master Hawkins had appeared to lose his mind—they feared he might take his own life. What would happen to them all?

Titus struggled to respond. He was sad, too, but then he raised himself up and said, "Not just de good ones dies, Stepney. De good Mistah Ray preached dat de rains falls on all of us, good an' bad. Ya remember Mistah Varny? He gots run over by his own cart, and he was a bad one."

The memory broke through Stepney's despair, and he laughed. Titus joined in the laughter and then said, "Stepney, ya straighten up now! If dis family gots any chance ta stay together, den some of us gots ta do what we can. Ya Molly be aw right. Ya climb on out dis hole, and go act like ya hurt ya arm and sit a spell. I'll finish dis damn hole myself."

Titus finished the hole and climbed out. He told the men to make themselves more presentable by cleaning up with the pail of water. Stepney grabbed the pail and quickly washed his face and hands and wet down his hair. He tried to straighten his ragged clothes, but they were beyond improvement—they were covered with holes and tears and stains. The sadness came over him again.

Titus called to him, instructing Stepney to go down to the house and tell the reverend they were ready. The thought of being with his Molly excited him, so he did not hesitate. When Stepney reached the house, he found the entire island had gathered there. The Reverend MacSparren was positioned at the head of the funeral. He approached MacSparren, bowed, and with his eyes lowered said, "Miz Elizabet's grave is done ready for ya, Mistah Reverend."

MacSparren replied, "Yes, thank you, my good Stepney. We shall begin."

Stepney walked to the back of the casket, thinking of when he had been sent to summon the Reverend Ebenezer MacSparren for the funeral. For the last two days, however, the reverend had been waiting for Joseph Hawkins to allow the burial to proceed.

The venerable island leader Captain Simon Ray was the lay preacher on Block Island, but the Reverend MacSparren of Conanicut, Rhode Island, periodically visited the island to provide the sacraments. He was a busy Anglican circuit minister who served Anglicans and non-Anglicans across the Providence plantations and Rhode Island colony.

He had explained to Stepney that unless they were able to proceed soon, he would have to return to the mainland to attend to the full schedule of services that was waiting for him.

Now all was ready. At the front of the procession was the short, round reverend, dressed in black and wearing a tall hat, and carrying a large leather-bound Bible. Accompanying the reverend was his slave, Pompey, who carried a round brass vessel at the end of a chain that had pungent incense billowing from it. They walked in front of the simple wooden casket that was carried by six of the Hawkins' male slaves.

Stepney took his place to the side of Joseph Hawkins, opposite from where his Molly was standing. She was supposed to assist her master up the hill, but now Stepney would be there for the two of them. Molly and Stepney supported Joseph as he stood directly behind the casket. Molly was of little real support, for she was steadily weeping.

Joseph Hawkins stood, disheveled and unshaven, with a cold, blank stare on his face. Stepney looked behind them to see the growing crowd of mourners. He recognized each of the island leaders with their families—the families of the first settlers from almost one hundred years earlier who still occupied land on the island; families named Ray, Sands, Rathbone, Rose, Tosh, and Dodge. Those who had settled on Block Island more recently but also held a significant place in the island community were there too; families named Littlefield, Beach, Mitchell, Mott, Paine, Hull, and Dickens. Many, if not all, of the remaining three hundred white citizens on the island continued to gather. The show of love and respect caused a knot to tighten in Stepney's throat. The remainder of the Hawkins' slaves waited patiently to follow in the rear.

Chapter Thirty

Though Quepag was annoyed at being tied up, he was fascinated as he watched the procession make its way slowly toward the gravesite. The sky was growing dark, and the wind began to swirl. As the procession neared the grave, the first raindrops fell on the casket. A few of the islanders had umbrellas and raised them to provide cover from the rain. Quepag could hear the raindrops slowly drumming on the top of the wooden box.

The slaves had straightened up the area and put the tools behind the bushes. Titus looked over at Quepag and realized the Indian was still sitting with his feet bound together. The slave quickly untied the boy's feet, but Quepag was angered when Titus then tied the rope around his waist and held the other end.

Quepag watched silently as the slow procession approached the gravesite. He looked at Titus; the slave swallowed hard as tears streamed down his face. The boy had experienced much loss in his own short life, but he knew that he didn't feel the same as the others who were gathered at the grave. He wondered what made him different from them. He decided that the strange funeral procession was a very sad thing.

The crude wooden box was laid down on timbers set across the grave opening, and Reverend MacSparren positioned himself at the head of the grave, with his slave, Pompey, next to him. Master Hawkins, with Molly and Stepney on each of his arms, stood at the opposite side of the grave.

Quepag had lost interest in whatever was taking place on the other side of the ridge. Now, he was fascinated with the ceremony. He was interested to see how the whites said good-bye to their dead. While still tied by the cord Titus was holding, Quepag climbed onto a large rock to look at the crowd.

By the time the reverend began the ceremony, the sky had grown very dark, and the wind had picked up. MacSparren opened the large book Quepag recognized as the one they called the Bible. The day had suddenly grown so dark that Quepag could see the preacher squinting as he struggled to read the large letters in the dim light.

As the preacher strained to see the words, a tremendous wind came rushing over the ridge behind him and blasted the group. Quepag was almost blown off the rock but grabbed Titus for support. The mighty gust caused the men to grab their hats and the women to hold down their long petticoats. An anxious murmuring spread through the crowd, as all fearfully looked up at the storm that was so suddenly upon them.

The cold wind began to snap and swirl like no island wind Quepag had ever experienced. It seemed as if the wind was like a large whip being cracked, pulling at the crowd. It seemed as though their clothes and even their very hair might be pulled from their bodies.

Reverend MacSparren's tall hat was blown off, exposing his shiny bald head. As he turned to grab for his hat, the great Bible flapped out of his hands like a large bird. It fell to the ground and teetered on the edge of the grave. MacSparren let out a high-pitched scream, and the whole crowd gasped.

The reverend's hat hit another man in the head, knocking his hat off, and the two hats went dancing down the hill. Several of Hawkins' slaves ran after the hats. Suddenly, a bolt of lightning cracked behind

MacSparren, and the sky opened up to torrential rains. The wind was now pelting the group with leaves and twigs. Several more hats were knocked off, and umbrellas were turned inside out and blew away. A few more slaves broke to try to recover the items.

Most of the funeral party dissolved into disorder as they scrambled down the hill, hurrying to get out of the elements. Many bumped into one another, tripping and falling over each other as they fled the storm. Some of the island's leading men helped the frail and elderly down the hill. Only MacSparren, Hawkins, and their slaves stayed by the gravesite.

Quepag thoroughly enjoyed the scene that unfolded before him. He was sure his grandfather had conjured up the storm as revenge for his grandson's being embarrassed by the black men and indentured by the whites. To the Indian, the wind and the rain were exciting, and it humored him to see how the islanders were so upset by it. He laughed out loud and clapped his hands over his head.

Titus pulled him down from the rock and untied him, saying, "You be silent and respectful, Injun."

Quepag immediately broke away, running up and over the ridge. As he came over the ridge, he looked for signs of the digging and guns and fighting he had heard coming from this direction earlier. Once on the other side of the ridge, Quepag made his way swiftly through thick, thorny brush to the bluffs. He came to a clearing and looked around. It was obvious someone had been working there. There were many footprints, and it looked like a large boulder had been moved. *Was this where they were digging?*

Quepag continued on to the bluffs, and as he broke through the heavy brush, he his eyes widened with surprise at what he saw out on the water. His attention was immediately drawn to his left as Quepag saw smoke from a campfire coming from the top of the island's tallest bluffs. *Who would bother to camp there?*

Quepag was startled to hear footsteps and the rustling of brush behind him. He turned, expecting to see Titus coming after him. He didn't want to go back to the Hawkins plantation, so he decided he would return to the Manisses village on the Great Salt Pond and tell his grandfather all he had seen and heard. His grandfather Sachem was very wise and would help him in his understanding.

Chapter Thirty One

Stepney held his breath. Like the reverend, he could not move. The thought of the large Bible falling into the grave was horrifying. *Could der be anything more blasphemous or offensive dan dat?* He was most fearful it would be he who would have to retrieve it. Stepney couldn't bear to go back into that hole, not with Miss Elizabeth hanging over it.

In the midst of the chaotic scene around them, the Reverend MacSparren stood staring down at the Bible. His slave, Pompey, finally dropped down and grabbed the book, just before it slipped into the hole.

All the others had run off, leaving MacSparren, Pompey, Joseph Hawkins, Molly, Stepney, and the other four slaves who had dug the grave. Throughout the melee and in the midst of this now-raging storm, Joseph had stood stone-faced, staring down at the box.

Stepney saw the reverend breathe a brief sigh of relief. He wondered whether the reverend would quickly finish the burial or bring the box back to the house until the storm was over. He knew MacSparren had to leave the island as soon as possible for other pressing matters, so Stepney wasn't surprised when the reverend began to quickly finish the sacrament.

The small group struggled to stand in place as they were soaked by the rain, while looking to MacSparren for direction.

The reverend picked up the Bible and yelled through the howl of the raging storm, "Our good and gracious God! Accept Thy dear Elizabeth into Thy hands. From dust Thy servant came, and dust Thy treasure shall return. Glory be to God the Father and Thy son Jesus Christ. Amen."

With the word "amen," MacSparren slammed the Bible shut and lumbered off down the hill with Pompey running behind him.

Joseph Hawkins stood in place, held up by Stepney and Molly. Stepney's fears about the demise of the Hawkins family had become more and more real as the catastrophe unfolded around the gravesite. He was now almost certain this would be the end.

His Molly had been upset by Miss Elizabeth's death, but Molly always had a strength about her. He and the others were counting on her strength to offer hope through this ordeal, but now she could barely stand in her grief; she wailed and clutched at her abdomen.

Molly's grief was so strong that Stepney thought there must be something else, other than Miss Elizabeth's death, that concerned her. His composure crumbled as he now felt sure she was going to lose their child. Through his tears, he cried out, "God, don't do dis! Don't ya take no more from us! God, not de chile!"

Joseph's face had been blank, and he seemed oblivious to all that was going on around him. Stepney feared Joseph might just crawl into the box with Elizabeth and let the slaves bury the two of them together. He was afraid that when they buried their good Miss Elizabeth, it might be a final death blow to their master.

His master stood staring at the coffin, without moving. But just when Stepney was preparing to help him and Molly down to the house, he called out in a strong voice that startled them. "Farewell, my beloved! Thou did not deserve to wait for this fool. Thou shan't be forgotten. I make a solemn oath to thee as we lay thee to rest. I shall make our son, whom you so desired to be named Alexander, to be a living monument to thy memory."

With those words, Molly collapsed to the ground in utter despair and grief. Joseph turned to the burial party and said, "You men be gentle with our Elizabeth. She must not be awakened from her peaceful rest."

Joseph and Stepney then helped Molly up from the ground and struggled through the driving elements to make their way down the hill. Stepney felt comforted by his master's words. He said that their lives would go on because of the newborn baby named Alexander.

Stepney wondered if this baby would be the hope for the family's future, but his thoughts were diverted to the immediate concern of getting the three of them back to the house in one piece.

Stepney wondered if it was what he had said at the gravesite about God saving the children that might have caused Master Joseph to snap out of his delirium. Joseph must have realized that a part of his beloved Elizabeth was still alive and struggling to survive in a crib back at the house. A glimmer of hope began to grow in Stepney's heart and mind.

As they reached the bottom of the hill, Stepney looked back over his shoulder. Titus and the others had already lowered the box into the grave and were shoveling the dirt and rock back into the hole. Their black silhouettes were revealed with each jagged lightning strike that crashed beyond the ridge.

Stepney felt better as he glanced back over his shoulder, with each step closer to the house and each shovelful of dirt he saw the slaves fill in the grave. Perhaps this family would survive after all. He was even willing to accept that if Molly lost his child, she was strong enough to bear another.

His confidence grew, and he assured himself that if the storm didn't blow everyone into the sea, it would pass and a clear sky would return. Maybe the good Miss Elizabeth would take their troubles with her. The Reverend MacSparren was right—she was a treasure, and she would now remain where she was. Hopefully, God would bless this family and this island for her goodness.

Stepney took one last look back and decided that the black silhouettes were not really working to bury the dead; they were actually building a sacred place of honor. He recalled an image from his childhood before he had been taken by the white men. For a moment, he could see again the stone mounds that had been built to remember the noble ancestors and great victories of his African tribe.

In the midst of the wild wind and driving rain, Stepney felt a calming peace come over him. He shook his head in astonishment that he could feel this way while the whole world around him seemed to be coming undone. It said to him that there was something out there that was greater than himself, greater than strong Titus, and even greater than Master Hawkins.

He wondered if this spirit was actually in control of all these events. A sudden revelation came to him—a revelation he could hardly dare to think was true. He softly muttered the question to whoever might be listening. "Could ya be makin' somethin' from all dis? Could ya be makin' somethin' good from all dis dat's so damnable bad?"

Chapter Thirty Two

The Mohegan Indian pirate Sachumjuia slipped away from the shore party and disappeared into the heavy forest. He had already made up his mind and departed with no intention of rejoining the crew until, perhaps, they returned. He had made plans to one day return to this island. It was because of this plan that he had directed Captain Gilcox to Manisses in the first place.

The Indian wove his way through the forest faster than most mortals could run on an open field, following the southern coastline eastward. The destination he had in mind was close at hand. When the Indian reached the southeast corner of the island, he stopped and surveyed the jagged clay and rock bluffs that dropped down to the rocky shore and into the vast ocean. Off to his right, he could see a storm brewing from the southwest. At the tall bluffs, where his forefathers had once fought, he gathered wood and built a fire. From a small pouch, he sprinkled a mixture of herbs, poppies, and gunpowder into the flames. They crackled and popped, developing a strong smoke that the Indian drew into his lungs.

He began to chant to the spirits. His chants were strained as he struggled to remember the words and the rhythms of the tribal elders.

He wished he had paid closer attention to those men at whom he used to scoff. He was a hunter and warrior, just like his father and his father's father before him. Now, at the place where his mighty forefathers died in battle, he desired to conjure up their spirits. It was a desire to feel close to them and to the heritage of his people, a closeness he had lost during his time spent out at sea. The Indian breathed deeply, closed his eyes, and chanted as best he could.

He began to feel himself rising up with the smoke and circling above the island. The freedom felt good, but he had a purpose, and his voice screamed out for words of knowledge from the fallen warriors. All at once, the wind that was lifting him up died, and he plummeted to the ground. He could feel his body slam down hard, leaving him flat on his back.

From behind his closed eyelids, it became pitch black, but he was soon enchanted by the bright splashes that appeared. Colors shimmered like those of the rainbow but even deeper and more vibrant. He was mesmerized by the colorful display when a bright white light suddenly burned all the color away. In the light stood the form of a man, who eventually stepped forward to reveal himself.

The Indian wanted to run forward to embrace the figure who he believed was his father, but he could not move. As the bright light dimmed, he could see his father amid the bushes adorned with brilliant wild pink roses. His father picked one of the blooms from the bush and put it in his mouth. He chewed on the flower as if it were a fully satisfying meal. With so many blooms around him, Sachumjuia wondered why he didn't eat more.

Suddenly, Sachumjuia felt a cold wind and harsh elements beat against him. He tried to ignore them and stay focused on his father. The cold wind caused the petals of the flowers to shrivel up and fall off the bushes until they were barren. Finally, he saw the image of his father start to shrivel up in the same fashion as the flowers, and his body became like the petals. Bit by bit, his body fell to the ground with the rose petals until he was gone.

The Indian tried to reach forward and catch the falling petals, but he couldn't move. His arms were pinned to his body. Sachumjuia wrestled to loosen himself, but couldn't move until the petals had all fallen. He then tore his arms free to beat his chest. He struggled to scream until a great wind surged from his lungs and a primal wolf howl escaped. His eyes bolted open, and he found himself sitting with crossed legs before the fire. Only now, a frenzied wind and rain was whipping up, and the burning fire had been scattered. Pieces of the wood were still burning, and many had blown right into the Indian's lap. He jumped up to brush away the burning wood and ash.

Sachumjuia's head was still cloudy from the smoke, so it took a second for him to recall where he was. Soaked by the heavy rain, he looked up from the fire and out over the high bluff. He saw something moving offshore and was certain that it must have been their ship, but there were no sails aloft or even any masts left standing. She was moving slowly southeast, out to the deep water and shrinking into the sea. Finally, she disappeared under the waves.

The question of what had happened to the ship did not even enter into his mind. The Indian began to jump and dance and chant again. These were not actions that came from anger or despair but from exhilaration. He immediately concluded that his connection to the spirits had been made. His forefathers had heard his chants. They had not only provided him with a dream as an answer to the future course of his life but had made certain that he would follow their instruction by sinking the ship. Now, he concluded that he must seek out a wise man to interpret his dream so that he might fulfill his destiny.

Sachumjuia headed into the forest to find shelter from the elements but then stopped. His mouth fell open and his eyes widened. Stepping forward, he knelt down and reached out to touch something that he was not sure was real. Grabbing the stem, he pulled it from the bush and brought it close to his face. There before him in the soaking rain was the bright pink wild beach rose from his dream. The sharp thorns from the stem confirmed that it was all too real. Beneath the pink flower, bright red blood dripped down his arm.

Chapter Thirty Three

As the three approached the house, Stepney saw that the remaining mourners had filled the house and were spilling out onto the porch. He was surprised to see several Manissean Indians talking to men on the porch and pointing toward the north.

Constable Simon Ray spotted them coming down from the hill and ran out into the storm to meet them. He called above the storm, "Joseph, you know how sorry I am for your grief. But our island has encountered another calamity. It has been but ten years since the wreck of the *Princess Augusta* out on the hummocks, and I'm afraid it has happened once again. The Indians gauge this ship to be another palatine ship but a smaller vessel of less than two hundred tons.

"We would desire to stay to comfort you, but I'm afraid it is urgent. She must have struck very hard because she is breaking up and on fire. The Indians say that this time the crew has abandoned the passengers and the poor souls on board are starved, needing to be carried off. I'm sorry, Joseph, but the men of Block Island must go."

Joseph immediately responded, "Yes, of course. The *Princess Augusta* has given us islanders a poor reputation as wreckers. Many people from the mainland accuse us of luring ships to wreck on our shores, but we know it is not so. We cannot let another wreck further tarnish our reputation. We know that there is no higher priority for islanders than to rescue those in distress. It is our duty. I must go, too. Elizabeth would have wanted me to help rescue those poor people. The Hawkins men will join you."

Joseph turned to Stepney. "Take Molly to the house and have one of our Negroes care for her and the child. Then, you come with Titus and the others in the wagon and the oxcart. Bring all the rope and blankets you can find." Turning back to the constable, he said, "Simon, let us gather the men together and ride out to the point."

Stepney was amazed at how this emergency had snapped his master back into the man of strength, bearing, and purpose he had been just a few days earlier.

~~~

The storm had quieted, but the wind and rain continued while the slaves raced to collect the rope and blankets and hitch up the wagon and oxcart. Stepney sat alongside Titus at the reins of the wagon. They didn't speak as they rode north along the oxcart path known as Center Road and then onto the Corn Neck cart path leading up to Sandy Point. Stepney could think of nothing but his Molly back at the house. All he wanted to do was to be with her, but he knew that would have to wait. If this wreck was truly anything like the *Princess Augusta*, this would be a very long day.

The wagon left the lumbering oxcart behind and rode past the Great Salt Pond, through Indian Head Neck, past the thick cornfields toward Chagum Pond. Suddenly, like a ghostly spirit, the woman Dutch Kattern, also called Long Kate, appeared by a long stretch of stone wall that ran along the cart path. She was partially hidden by a thicket and stood erect, staring off into the distance, seemingly unaffected by the wind and cold rain.

The two men quietly stared at her as they passed, until Stepney broke the silence. "I's afeared of dat lady. Does ya think she's a witch, as some do say, Titus? She always gettin' herself into a state and sayin' she been off visitin' her home country. Maybe she brought dis new palatine ship onta our rocks. Maybe dey's her family on dis boat. Maybe she done it."

Titus reasoned, "Long Kate ain't no witch; she's tetched, is all. How many ships done crashed on dis island? Ya think she been de cause of 'em all? No, dis is just another ship a storm done pushed onta our rocks."

"Does ya think dis will be as bad as de *Augusta*?"

Titus paused and then responded, "Dat *Princess Augusta* was a awful bad one. Da day was cold and snowy. Pullin' dem starved people off de ship and den seein' most of 'em froze solid on de beach was hard. It gave dis island a bad name. It was dat first mate, Brooke, who kilt de captain and starved dem poor souls. He was de devil. He done everything he could ta steal all dat was on da ship and den sink her. I hope by God dis one won't be as bad. At least it ain't as near frozen as dat day."

Stepney looked back at the Dutch woman and said, "Long Kate came off de *Augusta*, and she survived. Her and Short Kate was de only ones ta stay on de island. I heard Long Kate tells people's futures. Ain't dat what witches does?"

"No, she ain't no witch," Titus recalled, "but when Littlefield's slave, Newport, pulled her off de *Augusta*, she sure put a spell on him. Now he's livin' wid her and dey tellin' everybody dey's married. I sure enough don't know who done de ceremony. It makes a few on the island angry, but dey all just let 'em be. Dis ways de town faddas don't has ta worry 'bout if dey's goin ta have ta care fa Long Kate."

When the wagons came over the rise, they looked across Chagum Pond to the palatine ship that was listing and on fire. Stepney wearily exclaimed, "Good God."

Titus snapped the reins and yelled, "Ha!" The wagon rumbled across the bumpy dirt trail toward Sandy Point.

When they arrived at the site of the wreck, they gathered up blankets and went to cover those passengers lying on the cold beach. It seemed that most of them were dead already. The few who were alive spoke in the same Dutch language as the survivors of the *Princess Augusta*, except for one who spoke English in a coarse Dutch accent.

Stepney saw his master, Joseph, and called him over to the man to see if he could understand him. Joseph knelt down and asked, "What is it, man? What has happened to you? Your people looked starved. Where are the captain and crew? Where does this ship hail from?" The man only had enough strength to whisper, so Joseph leaned close to him, and then repeated what he heard to Stepney. "Scottish-built ship owned by the Dutch. Merchants and emigrants from German country bound for Philadelphia." Joseph probed further. "What happened, man? What happened?"

He repeated the man's answer: "Stormy crossing. Crew mutinied. They killed the captain and took the ship. Crew seized stores and arms and starved them to give up their money for food. When their money gave out, they were left to starve. Dead thrown into the sea."

Hawkins then asked, "What happened to the dastardly mutineers?" After listening to the man's answer, he repeated aloud, "Sighted land and escaped in longboats; left us to die. We were too weak to sail the ship, and she crashed. One tried to light a signal torch. Ship caught on fire."

Joseph began to ask another question, but the man's body began to shake and then suddenly went limp. Joseph simply said, "The poor soul's gone."

More and more islanders arrived at the scene, and they continued to steadily remove the passengers from the burning ship, both the living and the dead. After those who were alive were pulled off the ship, the men had to abandon their efforts. The sheet anchor was chopped free and the palatine ship was pulled off the hummocks by the rising tide.

The blazing ship, caught in the fierce riptide, began to dance wildly in its turbulence.

Stepney stood silently next to his master with the rest of the exhausted islanders, watching the unearthly light show. To Stepney, it seemed as though a large hand had grabbed hold of the ship from beneath the sea and was steadily pulling her out to the deep. The inferno grew brighter as the ship shrank in the distance. It appeared almost as a signal torch being waved back and forth. Slowly but steadily, the unseen hand pulled her straight down, extinguishing the fire in a huge puff of steam and smoke. The palatine ship was gone.

Standing amongst the dead and dying, Stepney wanted answers to his questions. What was all this? What was happening? He looked at the other islanders. They slowly and sadly began the task of gathering up the bodies. He turned to his master for answers. Joseph looked back at him and finally he broke down and wept. Stepney could not help himself—he, too, began to cry at the sadness embodied in all that had been lost that day. The dead and dying ship further opened up the emotions to their pent-up grief.

~~~

The cold, still bodies were loaded into the wagons. They moved slowly toward Captain Ray's home to the southeast of the island. The islanders agreed that the bodies would be buried in the same field where the *Princess Augusta*'s dead were buried. Stepney looked back as the wagons departed Sandy Point and simply shook his head. The debris from the palatine ship continued to wash up onto the stony beach.

Stepney was certain that Joseph Hawkins and the people of Block Island had lived through one of their worst days. They rode their wagons back to their homes, shaking from the cold rain. He knew that every islander, both slave and free, was feeling something of what he felt, like the palatine ship being devastated by rock and fire.

Stepney sullenly stared off at the stone wall that stretched on as he rode quietly alongside Titus. He then wondered aloud, "What hope does we have?", wanting Titus to say something to encourage him, but the older slave sat silently. Stepney's heart sank further.

As Stepney looked off he began to focus on one part of the wall a short distance ahead. The wall seemed to be moving. His curiosity turned to shock as a form began to emerge and take shape from the stones.

Stepney's eyes widened and a cold fear rose up within him as they drew closer. The form took shape and once again, the survivor of the *Princess Augusta*, Dutch Kattern, appeared right on Stepney's side of the wagon.

Stepney shifted in his seat toward Titus as they passed by her. The woman was soaked from the rain, and her hair hung down, hiding most of her face, and a large, dark cape covered her entire body. Stepney stammered, "Good God, Titus, if Long Kate ain't no witch, den I don't knows nothin'."

When they were alongside her, she raised her arm and pointed her finger right at Stepney. He clenched the wooden bench he was sitting on and pressed himself even closer against Titus.

She called out in a ghostly, halting voice, "Godt has told me—der woman is dead but der boy is alive. He lives!"

Stepney held his breath. He continued to stare at the woman with his mouth open and his eyes bulging.

She repeated, "He is alive! He is alive! He is alive!"

He could not take his eyes off of her until she disappeared behind them as they drove around a bend in the cart path. Stepney began to breathe again. The two slaves looked at each other and shook their heads in disbelief.

Stepney's heart still raced as he continued to hear the woman's haunting voice calling in his head. Then, to his surprise, once again, as it had earlier when he descended the hill from the burial, the same strange sense of peace washed over him. Long Kate was saying that the boy was alive. *Yes, of course, she was talking of de new Hawkins baby. What was de name? Oh, yes—Alexander. Dey named de baby Alexander. He be alive, and he will survive. Is he de hope for dis family?* That small ember of optimism began to softly glow again.

Stepney spoke aloud to encourage both himself and Titus. "It be aw right, Titus. De boy, Alexander, is alive. We be aw right."

Chapter Thirty Four

Like a great cataclysmic event of nature, Giddy Gilcox's world aboard the *Rogue Flattery* was suddenly shattered. In the howling wind, crashing lightning, and torrential rain, the ship began disintegrating before his eyes. The ship hit the great black rock dead on her bow. Everything on deck collapsed forward, and Giddy was thrown into the wheel so hard that he broke right through it. The steerage lines all snapped and wrapped around him like octopus tentacles. The rest of the crew was either crushed or trapped beneath the masts, sails, and rigging.

Giddy could hear the fruitless cries for help of the few who were still alive. The ship, pushed off the rock by the storm, continued out into the deeper water and swiftly filled with the sea through the massive hole in her bow.

Giddy struggled to get free and was able to twist around into a sitting position, but he could not free himself completely. After several minutes of desperate struggle, he was able to free one of his arms, but there was nothing to grab for leverage to pull himself out. The cries of the other men died out. The bow of his beloved ship was now under water, and the rising sea was drawing closer and closer. Since the time he had left England, Giddy had been master of his own destiny, and he loathed the idea that his power was coming to an end.

Flashes of memory pulsed through his head as the frothy brine crept closer. First, Black Sam Bellamy came to mind. Like Black Sam's demise, surely this was the result of the black evil from the slave ship that they had scuttled months earlier. He had resisted the crew's superstitions, but now it all seemed beyond coincidence. The same slave ship curse that had dragged Black Sam down with *Whydah* was now dragging him down, too.

Suddenly, the thought of his father came to his mind. The dried carcass of Nigel Gilcox was still tied to the chair in the hold below him. When Giddy and his crew had absconded with the *Righteous Gale*, the mutineers had taken Mr. Gilcox down below and tied him to a chair. Giddy hadn't yet decided what to do with his father when he went to the hold where his father was bound to the chair. The senior Gilcox recognized instantly that Giddy was behind the mutiny and began berating his son, just as he had done when Giddy was a child. Only moments before, Giddy had decided never to let others abuse him again. His father's harsh words, he then decided, would be the final humiliation. Without thinking, he ripped off a large piece of cloth, wadded it up, and stuffed it into his shocked father's mouth. It was jammed in so tight that the elder Gilcox could not remove it, and he started to choke. Giddy then turned to find a sack and emptied its contents. He put the sack over his father's head, and with some rope, tied it tightly around his neck. His father would live the rest of his life—as short as that may have been—finally knowing what Giddy had lived with for most of his life.

Against his crew's objections, Giddy left his father there to rot and decompose. While Giddy never entered that hold again, the sight provided a constant reminder to the crew of exactly what their captain was capable of.

As the wind howled and the hull groaned, Giddy's thoughts turned to the woman and her boy. It occurred to him that all three were likely covered by the sea below him. The woman had caused Gilcox exceeding anxiety, and she had often entered his mind. He toyed with the idea that the strange way she looked at him back on the British man-of-war meant that she fancied him. At one point during the voyage north, he decided that he had to find out and so he brought her to his cabin, only to discover that her look was one of pity and nothing more.

Of all the abuse he had taken throughout his life, this woman's pity seemed to hurt the most. He wanted to kill her for that, but something stopped him from dealing the fatal blow. He then decided it was for the best, for he still needed the hostages alive until their treasure was hidden. But what had intervened to spare the life of this woman?

The cross! Yes, the cross. It had caught his eye the instant he was held back from killing her. Was there some supernatural or spiritual life in that charm? Was there some power in the cross?

Power in the cross? He had heard those words before. But where? He did not believe in spiritual things, and religion had never been a part of his upbringing. The only people he knew who were religious were weak and two-faced. But still, something had happened. It had caused him to consider that there was, indeed, some strange power in the cross she wore. He had snatched it from her neck and kept it on his person to see if he might wield its power.

Blast! The cross! he thought.

Gilcox felt for the gold charm in his pocket. And where was it now? Oh, yes, he had left it on the island. Why hadn't he clung to the cross for his own safety? Suddenly, his mind flashed farther back—what were the familiar words the woman hostage sang from the hold? Twice he had come to the door, in spite of his father's presence, intending to enter to discover more about the woman, but twice he had turned away. The hymns from the woman's sweet voice drifted through the door and took him back to a time that he had erased from his mind.

As he listened from the door, he heard his own mother's beautiful voice singing to a small, beloved child before he had been disfigured. The memory stabbed at his heart for the cruelty of a conditional love that couldn't see the same child trapped behind a physical affliction.

The song's words were so hauntingly familiar that he found he could not face the woman while she sang them. It suddenly dawned on him where he'd heard the words before. He was transported to a time somewhat later in his childhood, while hiding in the back of the old church.

Giddy's family was not religious and had never attended church, but the old church was the one location where Giddy could hide from his tormentors. On one particular Sunday, he'd hid during an afternoon service. In the security of his nook, he ignored the ceremony going on in the church sanctuary, but at some point, he began to listen to the hymns. Suddenly, he heard a man speaking to him and inviting him to come forward to receive a gift. Giddy was well hidden, but now he was sure he had been discovered and that the preacher was talking directly to him.

He listened to the old pastor's words. "Yes, a gift—a gift of God's grace. For you! Yes, you there! You, who are downtrodden, abused, and afflicted. A gift free to you but bought by a Savior's death on the cross!" He spoke of man's need for love, caring, and affection with no conditions. "For a love that gives and forgives, unconditionally, you need to cling to the cross. There is power in the cross!"

With the thought of the cross pulsing though his brain, his vision was struck again by the light from the woman's neckpiece. The light became a lightning bolt that cracked in front of him, jolting him back to the present and his sinking ship. The end on board the *Rogue Flattery* was drawing closer. For the first time Giddy could ever remember, he feared death. He found himself pining for the only place of warmth and security he could remember. He shut his eyes to send himself back to the old church.

In the church, he heard the call to him and felt drawn to come out of his hiding place. As he rose and stepped out to go forward and accept this beautiful gift, his heart was suddenly filled with indignation. There, stepping before him, was Ian Woodrow, the biggest offender of heaping ridicules, insults, and physical abuse upon him over the years. This cruel and heartless brute was now stepping forward to seek the same gift that had been offered to Giddy.

Giddy felt that it was he, himself, who was the victim. How could God possibly offer the same gift to the tormentor as the victim? He decided right then that all the others didn't deserve forgiveness and, as the victim, he certainly didn't need it. It was the world that had abused him!

At that point, his anger fueled him to harden his heart. God was so freely forgiving of what Giddy felt should never be forgiven. Giddy slipped out the back of the church, determined that if God wouldn't do it, then he would exact his own measure of revenge, and Ian Woodrow would get his full portion. He never returned to the church again.

Now, Giddy's mind awoke to the feel of the icy waters surrounding his legs. The ship groaned as her hull swelled with the cold sea. He felt the same indignation he had felt years earlier. Even as he pirated, robbed, lied, and murdered, in his mind, he was still the victim, and this unknown God was robbing him of a life's worth of vengeance.

He had never prayed or tried to speak to God before, but now, with the rising waters swallowing him up, Giddy Gilcox chose to shake his fist to the heavens and scream curses at God for the unfairness of it all. His screams cut to quiet as he and his mistress slipped below the surface on their descent down to their murky hell.